Zac and the Dream Stealers

Zac and the Dream Stealers

by Ross MacKenzie

Chicken House

Scholastic Inc. • New York

For Willie, Bunty, Margaret,
and George — and grandparents everywhere.
Your magic stays with us forever.

1

Zac Wonder sprinted through the forest, the carpet of
frozen leaves crunching beneath his bare feet. Whatever
was chasing him was gaining.

He leapt over a fallen branch and skidded to a halt at
the edge of a deep ravine. There was no way across. He
was trapped. The trees rustled, and he whirled around.

A tall figure in black stepped out into the moonlight.
In place of a face was a gleaming silver skull. Its arms,
encased in bone-shaped silver armor, were folded across
its chest.

Zac felt panic rise in his throat as the terrifying appa-
rition advanced toward him. Without thinking, he took a
fatal step backward, and fell, tumbling into darkness . . .

He landed with a thud on the living-room floor.

"Another one, lad?"

Zac sat up with a start at the sound of his grandmother's voice. Perched on her rocking chair by the fire, she was gazing at him over her newspaper.

He nodded, rubbing his eyes.

Another one. Another bad dream.

"You all right?" she asked.

"I dreamt I was being chased by a skull and crossbones. How stupid is that?" he said, trying to sound casual, but his heart was racing.

She stared at him hard for a second, then turned back to her paper. Zac could have sworn her hands shook slightly.

He clambered clumsily back onto the couch and lay there, thinking. Tall and gangly for an eleven-year-old, Zac had large, awkward feet, crystal blue eyes, and a mop of messy brown hair that always tickled his forehead.

Tonight was the sixth time in a week he'd woken up shivering and afraid. These days it seemed to happen every time he went to sleep. And he wasn't alone. Every day the television news reported the spread of bad dreams. It was like an epidemic.

The world was changing. People were scared.

Zac cast a sideways glance at his grandmother. Granny Wonder was tiny and round, with a cloud of silver hair. She always kept two pairs of golden spectacles on a string of pearls around her neck — one for reading and the other for distance. Puffing away on her favorite pipe, she was squinting at the paper with such concentration it looked as though she were trying to read using the wrong glasses. Zac took a peek at the front page to find out what was so fascinating. SCARED TO DEATH! screamed the headline: NIGHTMARES ON THE INCREASE AS CRIME WAVE BATTERS BRITAIN!

When she'd finished reading, Granny hissed through her teeth and tossed the paper into the fire, shaking her head. The pages wrinkled and blackened in the flames.

Granny had never been completely normal. She'd always whispered to the birds in her backyard and smoked that awful pipe. The other children were scared of her. They said she was a witch. A witch! Zac shook his head at the thought, and rubbed the ugly bruise under his eye — the latest result of defending Granny's honor at school. He didn't care how many black eyes he got, or that his classmates whispered when he walked past. He wouldn't swap Granny for a hundred friends. She was all he'd ever known. After Mum had died, and Dad had ditched him, Granny had given him everything. Even so, Zac couldn't deny she'd changed these past few weeks.

It had started around the same time as the reports about bad dreams began. She'd become extremely quiet, and though Zac would have been the first to admit Granny had never been a chatterbox, this was different. She'd barely said two words for weeks.

She'd also begun exercising. She only did it when she thought nobody was watching, of course, but Zac had caught her doing jumping jacks in the backyard twice that week. He'd even seen her trying one-armed push-ups.

Lastly, and most intriguing of all, Granny Wonder had been disappearing every single night at the stroke of midnight.

What was she *doing*?

Zac had made up his mind. Granny was up to something, and he was going to find out what.

Tonight.

2

As the grandfather clock in the hall struck midnight, Zac lay curled up in bed, doing his very best impersonation of someone who was fast asleep. A storm was building, and the wind rattled his bedroom window.

Creak.

That was Granny's door. She was right on time.

Zac heard her stop outside his room. The door opened a fraction. He closed his eyes tightly and concentrated on breathing slowly. He even threw in the occasional sleepy snort.

Creak.

The door closed again. Zac breathed a sigh of relief as Granny made her way downstairs. Then he leapt into action, throwing on his robe and slippers, and sneaking toward the door. He pressed his ear against the wood.

Silence.

Zac held his breath, reached down, and delicately turned the doorknob. The latch clicked open and he pulled the door gently inward.

The hallway was pitch-black; darkness clung to everything like tar. Zac shivered as he crept toward the stairs. The old house was *freezing*. It didn't help that his pajamas were two inches too short, which meant a chilly breeze was wafting up his pants legs.

He descended the stairs. It was a little easier to see here, because the glass on the front door let in a long sliver of orange light from the streetlamp. The kitchen was at the back of the house, so Zac tiptoed down the hall, carefully avoiding the creaky floorboards. A lifetime of sneaking downstairs for midnight snacks had taught him a useful lesson!

The kitchen was deserted. Zac crept to the window and looked out at the backyard. A blizzard was blowing with gusto; he could barely see the end of the garden. As he wiped the condensation from the glass, he caught a glimmer of movement. Yes, there it was again! Through the curtain of falling snow he could just make out a figure . . .

It was Granny, struggling with all her might against the wind.

Zac was dumbfounded. He blinked. Was he still asleep? What on earth was she doing out in a snowstorm in the middle of the night?

Transfixed, he watched Granny reach the frozen goldfish pond in the middle of the garden. She stopped at the edge and glanced around. Zac ducked out of sight. Seconds later he looked again, and what he saw made his hair stand on end.

Granny was jumping into the pond!

As she disappeared under the icy surface, Zac screamed in shock. He had to do something! He turned, ran straight into the kitchen table, ignored the flash of pain, and sprinted to the door. Tying the belt of his robe tightly, he threw himself out into the storm.

The bitter cold hit him immediately, wrapping an icy hand around his throat, squeezing the air from his lungs. On he charged, fighting against the stinging wind and snow. The wind howled in his ears and whipped great flakes of snow into his eyes.

Granny Wonder still hadn't emerged from the fishpond. Zac felt his heart thundering as he covered the final few steps to the water's edge. He half expected to find her lifeless body floating there, but there was nothing but a large hole in the thin layer of ice. Zac's mind raced. How could someone just disappear into a shallow fishpond? Shielding his eyes from the blizzard, he frantically looked around the garden. Where was she? He searched for footprints that might lead away from the water's edge, but there were none. Granny clearly hadn't climbed out.

"*Follow her in.*"

What was that? Zac spun a full circle. No one was there.

"*Follow her in.*"

Someone was whispering.

"*Into the pond,*" the voice said again.

"No way!" yelped Zac—just as a powerful gust of wind knocked him from his feet. He sailed through the tumbling snowflakes, watching with horror as the icy surface of the pond drew nearer and nearer . . .

He braced himself for the sting of freezing water, but when he crashed through the ice, the pond was warm! It felt just like a relaxing bath. He trod water for a moment, listening to the wind, now a ghostly whisper, and the magnified sound of his own heartbeat. Granny's goldfish tried to nibble his fingers. Then, almost as though someone had pulled a plug at the bottom of the pond, he was sucked down . . .

Zac landed hard on a cold stone floor. As he lay on

his back, trying to catch his breath, he realized not a bit of him was wet, even though he'd fallen into a fishpond. Things were getting *really* strange now!

Above his head was the surface of the pond. It looked as though a layer of water was suspended in the air. Astonished, he realized he could still see the goldfish swimming in it, as if they didn't mind the gaping void beneath them. He could even see the swirling blizzard. It was like looking up through a liquid skylight. To one side of the suspended pond he spotted a rickety wooden ladder, which seemed to be the only way back to the surface. Useful — but first he needed to find Granny.

Turning, he realized he was at the entrance to some sort of stone chamber. Taking a breath, he crept in.

The air in the chamber was thick with dust, and smelt like snuffed candles. Enormous cobwebs sparkled like diamond necklaces by the light of a fire popping in the hearth. Books covered every inch of the walls. In the very center of the chamber stood a crumbling stone archway, leaning to one side as though it were tired as well as ancient. It looked very odd standing there on its own.

"Hello, lad."

Zac's heart leapt, and he spun around to see Granny sitting in a comfortable armchair, peering at him over her golden glasses. On her lap she balanced a book so large her legs were entirely hidden.

"You're OK!" said Zac. "When I saw you jumping into that pond . . ."

"I'm fine," she said apologetically. "I'm sorry if I scared you. I wasn't entirely sure you'd follow me through the ice, so I made the wind give you a little push. I hope you don't mind."

Zac frowned. "You knew I was following? You wanted me to come here? Why? What's going on? What is this place?"

"Well now," she said, "that's the million-dollar question, isn't it?" She heaved the enormous book up onto a chunky table, and leaned back in her armchair. "You'd better sit down," she continued.

Zac flopped into the armchair next to her. His mind was spinning.

"I'm going to tell you something, lad," she said, "something very important. In fact, it's the biggest secret there is to tell."

3

When Granny next spoke, her voice was barely more than a whisper.

"What do you know about dreams, lad?"

Zac thought for a moment. "Am I dreaming *now*?" he asked.

"That depends on how you look at it," said Granny. "Let me put it another way. Where do you go when you dream?"

Zac scratched his chin. After some consideration, he said, "I don't go anywhere. I'm asleep when I dream."

"Aha!" said Granny, punching the air. "Your body is asleep. But what about the rest of you?"

Zac looked down at his robe and pajamas. "There isn't any more of me," he said.

Granny laughed. "What about your spirit, Zac?" she exclaimed. "What about the bit of you that makes you *you*? It has to go somewhere while your body is resting, doesn't it? Otherwise it'd get bored and shrivel up, like a raisin!"

Zac stared at Granny. She appeared to be serious. He knew his mouth was hanging open, but he couldn't seem to do anything about it.

"Granny," he began, "are you telling me that when I'm sleeping . . . a bit of me goes off somewhere else? And that's what a dream is?"

Granny produced her pipe from her cardigan and lit it. She took several puffs, and feathery wisps of smoke tickled the air. "Almost."

"Where?" he said. "Where does it go?"

"To another world, on the other side of sleep — a place called Nocturne," whispered Granny. "Actually, to a place *within* the land of Nocturne . . . somewhere called the Dream Plains. That's where everyone's spirit goes to play."

"Granny?"

"Yes, lad?"

"Are you pulling my leg?"

"I've never been so serious about anything," she said solemnly.

"How do you know about this? About Nocturne?" said Zac.

"I used to live there."

"You what?"

"I know it's hard to believe, but you'd better start," said Granny, "because terrible events in Nocturne are about to spill over into your world—the Waking World—and when that happens, there'll be no going back."

"This is too weird," said Zac, scratching his head nervously.

Granny tapped the end of her pipe against her teeth. "Look, just let me explain. It all started many years ago, when a group of people left the Waking World and traveled to Nocturne. We don't know how they discovered its existence, or how they managed to get there, because it was long before the Gateway was built." She pointed to the crumbling arch in the center of the room. "When they arrived, they found that the whole of Nocturne was naturally charged with powerful magic — the magic that spills out of the dreams of Wakelings."

"Whatlings?" said Zac.

"Wakelings — people from the Waking World," Granny said. "Anyway, this group of travelers — the Nocturne Founders — realized they could harness this magic. But some of them wanted greater magical powers, and they soon realized that they could harness bad dreams more easily than good dreams. So they began to interfere with the dreams of Wakelings."

"What did they do?" Zac asked, bobbing up and down in his chair.

Granny scrunched up her face as though she'd just got a whiff of fresh dog poo. "They twisted Wakeling dreams into nightmares. It did make their magic stronger. But it was a dark magic fed by the misery of others."

"That's terrible!" exclaimed Zac.

"These dark magicians call themselves Dream Stealers," said Granny, "and that's just what they are — they hijack dreams. They've been kept at bay for many years but now they're coming back, and they're growing stronger with every night that passes. Their dark magic is poisoning the dream world — and it's weakening the Knights. If we're going to have any chance of stopping them, we must act quickly. There's no other way. We leave for Nocturne tonight."

"Wait. Whoa! What?" said Zac. "What do you mean?"

"Weren't you listening?" said Granny. "There's no time to waste!"

"But are you *sure* we aren't safe here in the Waking World?" asked Zac.

"I wish we were," said Granny, shaking her head. "But that's not how it works. The more Dream Stealers there are, the more Wakelings will be tortured by terrible dreams. Nobody is safe, because everyone must sleep."

"Is that what's been going on?" breathed Zac. "All the bad dreams I've been having . . . the reports on the news about the same thing happening all over the country . . . it's all because of Dream Stealers?"

Granny nodded. "If they get their way," she said, "all dreams will turn to darkness. Zac, can you imagine what life would be like, knowing that you *must* sleep, but that whenever you do, you'll be tortured by your worst fears? People will be driven to do terrible things — the Waking World will be thrown into chaos."

"But what can we do to help?" said Zac. "You're old and I don't have any magic powers."

"How do you know?" asked Granny with a glint in her eye. "Listen, Zac, until now, the Dream Stealers have been held back by a group of *good* magicians known as the Knights of Nod. I happen to be one of them. Anyway, I'm not leaving you here alone while I go gallivanting off on some adventure!" Granny pointed to the crumbling archway. "Every night for the last few weeks, I've been meeting the Grandmaster of the Knights here. His name is Rumpous Tinn, and he's been keeping me up-to-date. There's a secret reason I've been away from Nocturne for so long, but tonight, he's taking me home."

"Oh," said Zac faintly. His head felt as if it were about to burst.

Granny ruffled his hair, making it stick up. "Don't worry," she said. "I'll look after you. Have I ever let you down?"

Zac shook his head. She never had.

As they sat, both deep in thought, the Gateway began to rumble. Tiny pieces of rubble fell to the floor. The room began to shake. Books tumbled from their shelves. Zac gripped his armchair so tightly his fingers grew numb. All at once there was a strange heat and a smell of hot metal, then a blinding light radiated from the Gateway, spitting two figures clean across the chamber. They landed in a tangled heap.

Zac turned to Granny, but before he could speak, she'd grabbed his arm and hit the floor, dragging him behind one of the armchairs. By the look on her face, something was very wrong.

"What's happening?" he whispered.

"We've got a problem, lad," she said. "Neither of those men is Rumpous Tinn."

4

Rumpous Tinn, Grandmaster of the Knights of Nod, was somewhere altogether different.

He could make out lights twinkling overhead, cutting through the fog in his mind. After a while, he felt strong enough to sit up. His entire body ached.

He was sitting on the stone floor of a small square room. There was a silver door in the corner which was covered in intricate gilding. Torches hung in delicate silver holders, the flickering torchlight reflected in a crystal chandelier. Tinn frowned and pulled his white robe tightly around him. Where *was* he?

The last thing he could remember clearly was being attacked in the Eternal Forest. There had been voices all around him, and he had managed to deflect a number of Dream Stealer hexes. But they had been coming at him from all sides.

He stood and hobbled over to the door. The decoration was quite beautiful with floral patterns and flourishes everywhere. Tinn caught his reflection in the gleaming silver. He looked old and tired. There wasn't a single hair left on his shining head, but he made up for this with a huge white beard that covered his chin from ear to ear. He sighed. The magic battle had sapped his energy much more quickly than he'd expected. The Dream Stealers were indeed growing stronger.

An awful thought struck him, and he began to pat his beard. After a second or two of searching, his fingers touched the thing he was feeling for, and he closed his eyes in relief. So the Dream Stealers hadn't found it. Well, that was something. But then, why hadn't they just killed him? The reason couldn't be good. Tinn decided it would be wise to escape.

He reached for the door handle.

BANG!

Tinn spiraled backward through the air, landing hard on the polished stone. He felt as if his bones were on fire. Panting, he pulled himself up onto an ornate iron chair — the only piece of furniture in the room — and examined his hand. His palm was badly burnt. He grimaced. There were no windows, no other doors. He was a prisoner.

"Well, old man," he said to himself, "good luck getting out of this one alone."

"You ain't alone," said a small voice, seemingly from nowhere.

Tinn leapt up amazingly quickly for a man of his years. His eyes searched the room for any sign of life. There was nothing. Perhaps he'd been hit on the head harder than he'd thought.

"I know what you're thinking," said the voice, "but you ain't imagining me."

"Show yourself!" demanded Tinn.

Silence.

"Show yourself, I say!"

"Why should I?" snapped the voice. "Them Dream Stealers, they're chomping at the bit to get their hands on me. They call me a ghost. Or a demon."

Tinn's eyes widened. "Which are you?" he asked.

"I ain't neither." But before the voice could elaborate, the sound of footsteps echoed in the corridor. "Sshh. They're coming back . . ."

Tinn felt something brush past him. "Wait!" he yelled. "Who are you?"

There was no answer. The door flew open, and two black-clad figures swept toward him. Silver skull masks covered their faces, and bone-shaped silver armored their forearms and hands, which were crossed over their chests. Dream Stealers: each one a walking skull and crossbones. One raised a hand and brought something heavy down hard across Tinn's face.

Dull pain coursed through the old man's head, and he fell into darkness once more.

5

Zac peeked around the armchair at the two men as they stumbled to their feet, clearly disoriented after coming through the Gateway.

Granny carefully lifted her spare set of gold spectacles from around her neck and began unscrewing one of the arms.

"What are you doing?" hissed Zac.

"Getting ready," said Granny. The arm was now completely separated from the spectacles. She held it in her hand and put the remainder of the glasses into one of her cardigan pockets. "Stay here. Keep out of sight. And if anything should happen to me, you climb up the ladder to the surface of the pond and don't stop running until you're safe. Understand?"

"But—"

"Do you understand?"

Zac felt sick. He managed to nod.

Granny gave him a wink, then leapt out from behind the chair and flicked the arm of her spectacles at the two men like a tiny wand. There was a flash of purple, and a huge glowing net spread across the room, wrapping itself around the intruders, who toppled to the floor in a wriggling package.

Granny stood over them, her hand raised. "Who are you?" she demanded.

The astonished face of an old man stared back at her through the net. He had a bushy, ginger-gray mustache, and wore a crushed cowboy hat and a long black coat.

"Identify yourself!" yelled Granny, brandishing the arm of her glasses again.

"Evegenia, it's me! Cornelius!"

"Cornelius?" said Granny. "Cornelius who?"

"Huggins!" answered the man, squirming madly. "Cornelius Huggins, remember?"

Granny lowered her hand slightly. "Where is Rumpous Tinn?" she said.

"He's been taken, Eve," replied the old man. "We were attacked by Dream Stealers in the Eternal Forest. Tinn distracted them long enough for us to escape. We came straight here."

"I can't feel my legs!" whimpered the other person in the net.

Granny moved closer, staring at the old man's face. Her eyes suddenly lit up. "Cornelius!" she exclaimed. "It really is you!"

"I told you!" said the man. "Let me out, before my old bones seize up!"

Granny flicked the arm of her glasses once more, and the net disappeared.

The old man in the cowboy hat sprang up and stood before her, his arms wide. "Eve Wonder!" he said. "By the stars, it's good to see you!"

"You, too, Cornelius," said Granny. "Sorry about that. Can't be too careful. I didn't recognize you under that mustache. It's been so long."

"Fifty years!" bellowed Cornelius. "Tinn only told us you were alive a few months ago. The shock almost killed me!"

The second man stood up beside him. He was much younger than Cornelius, and wore a long blue velvet jacket covered with stars, and thick glasses that magnified his eyes hugely. He reminded Zac of an owl.

"This is Julius," said Cornelius.

"How do you do," said Granny, sticking out a hand.

"I'm Evegenia Wonder. My friends call me Eve. And this is Zac. Now, what's happened? You say the Dream Stealers have Tinn?"

"They came out of nowhere," said Julius. "I don't know how they knew we'd be in the forest, but they surrounded us. If it hadn't been for Tinn, we'd have been taken, too."

"We must get him back," said Granny. "Without Tinn, we don't have a chance against a new wave of Dream Stealers."

"Agreed," said Cornelius.

"Then let's get going," said Granny.

Zac eyed the miniature wand. "Honestly, Granny, when I think of all the times I've been in fights at school because someone called you a witch," he muttered. "I could have saved myself a few beatings if I'd known they were right." He touched the purple bruise around his eye.

"Well, you know now," said Granny with a chuckle. "Anyway, I'm a magician, not a witch. Here, let me fix that. Magic can heal little cuts and bruises quite easily."

She flicked her wand and Zac felt a strange sensation, like warm honey, on his face. A moment later, the feeling was gone. Zac picked up a silver paperweight from among the scattered books on the desk. He peered at his warped reflection. The bruise had all but disappeared.

"Wow, thanks!" he said.

"I'm sorry I didn't fix that sooner, lad," said Granny, "but I couldn't very well go mending every little injury you ever had with magic, could I? Someone would've noticed."

Zac rubbed his cheek, and looked at the crumbling arch. "Are we *really* going through there?" he said.

"Yes," said Granny. "That's the Gateway between the Waking World and Nocturne. But before we go through, there's something you must know. Something important."

"What is it?"

"The Gateway is a dream arch. In a way, you'll be dreaming when we go through it. It's quite dangerous."

Zac raised his eyebrows. "Dangerous?"

"Yes," said Granny. "It'll show you a vision, something that'll try to tempt you into staying. Don't fall for it. If you get trapped in the Gateway, you'll be left floating somewhere between asleep and awake forever."

"You really know how to put someone's mind at rest, don't you?" said Zac.

"This is no joke," she snapped. "You mustn't stop. Understand?"

Zac stared into the old woman's eyes. She looked scared. "I promise," he said.

She hugged him so tightly he thought his ribs would pop, and then released him, turning to the Gateway. She took her little wand, tapped the stone three times, and the arch was filled with golden light.

Julius approached it first, but faltered as he reached the boundary. Cornelius coolly walked up behind him and gave him a shove in the back, and he flapped through the Gateway and out of sight. Then Cornelius turned and waved his hat at Zac before calmly strolling through.

"Your turn, Zac," said Granny. "Come on."

Zac edged forward. The closer he came to the Gateway, the more electrically charged the air seemed to be. He felt the arch drawing him in, as if it were a powerful magnet and he a shaving of iron.

By the time he stood next to Granny at the Gateway's edge it was a physical effort to resist its pull. But the golden light was warm and calming, and as it embraced him he felt safe; he felt happy.

Granny put her hand on his shoulder. "Don't fight it," she said. "Just let go. And remember, lad, keep walking. No matter what you encounter, it won't be real. I'll see you on the other side."

Zac looked at Granny, wondering whether this would be the last time he'd see her wrinkled face. He turned back to the Gateway, shielding his eyes.

"You can do it, lad, I know you can!"

He took a deep breath. And then, with Granny's words of encouragement still ringing in his ears, he walked bravely forward.

Immediately, his spirits lifted. He felt pleasure, excitement, and contentment all at once. It was as though he had been wrapped in a cotton-candy cocoon of happiness.

The warming light surrounded him. It enveloped him. It was a part of him.

A figure appeared from nowhere, floating serenely toward him.

As the shape drew nearer, Zac could see it was a woman. Her skin was like the glow of the moon and her hair tumbled around her beautiful face like ribbons of silk.

Captivated, Zac recognized her, not from memory, but from photographs. The joy that engulfed him now was so intense he thought he would burst.

"Mum?" he whispered.

She smiled back at him. She looked like an angel.

"I've been waiting to meet you, Zac," she said. Her voice was soft and distant.

He felt an overwhelming urge to hug her and never let go. But then he heard Granny's voice ringing in his ears: *"No matter what you encounter, it won't be real."*

"Come with me, Zac," murmured the vision.

Zac stood for a moment, mesmerized. He was so close. He wanted more than anything to take her hand and go with her. But he also knew it was a trick, a cruel deception to tempt him to stay.

He opened his mouth to say something, but there was a lump in his throat. A burning feeling spread from his chest to his eyes, and hot tears trickled down his cheeks. With a deep breath he wiped his face and managed to utter the most difficult words he'd ever had to say.

"I have to go."

"You can't go, darling," said his mother.

Zac spoke again, this time more forcefully. "I can't stay," he said. He thought of Granny, and, as he pictured her face, the vision released some of its hold on him. "This isn't real. You're not real. I wish you were, but you're not."

Fighting every instinct, he walked past the image

of his mother, then looked over his shoulder. She was watching him with a confused expression.

"Come back," she said.

Zac closed his eyes and thought of Granny again. She needed him. Thinking of her gave him strength. He turned away.

As he did, there was a horrible ripping noise. Zac looked back once more and felt a lurch of horror. The vision of his mum was changing. She was shrinking, becoming hunched and twisted. Her skin was rotting before his eyes, falling off the bone. Zac turned and ran, almost tripping over his own feet. The monster followed. She was fast. Gasping for air, Zac pushed himself on, but he was running too quickly. He slipped, tumbling to the floor. The terrible, zombielike ghoul stooped over him, shedding chunks of flesh. Her flaking face grew closer and closer, until it pressed against his skin. He screamed.

"Zac?"

"Is he all right, Eve?"

"I don't know. Zac? Zac! Open your eyes, lad, come on!"

"Mum?"

"Look! He's waking up!"

"He is! He is! He's waking up!"

Zac's vision was fuzzy. He felt as though he'd been

dropped on his head. Peering down anxiously at him were the blurred faces of Granny, Cornelius, and Julius.

He sat up, and Granny gave him another rib-crunching hug.

"Good lad!" she said, tears filling her pearly gray eyes once more. "I knew you could do it. I'm so proud of you!"

"It was Mum," said Zac, and the rotting face flashed in his mind. "When I tried to get past, she turned into . . . some kind of zombie."

Granny exchanged a grave look with Cornelius. "This is bad," she said. "Like anything magical, the Gateway draws its protective power from the Dream Plains. I expected it to try to trick you with what you dream of most, but not to twist it into something so truly terrible. Things must be far worse than we thought. The Dream Plains are being taken over Zac, I'm so sorry you had to go through that. I'd never have put you in such a position if I'd known. Are you all right?"

"I think so," he said. "It seemed so real for a minute, and then . . ." He shook the vision from his mind. "It doesn't matter. I've made it."

Granny helped him up.

"Zac, are you sure you're OK?" said Julius. It was the first time he'd spoken to him.

"I'm fine. Thanks. Aargh! What's that?"

Zac leapt back from Julius, who seemed to be holding

a small ball of fire in his hand. Amused, Granny and Cornelius looked on as though it was the most normal thing in the world.

Julius gazed blankly at Zac for a moment, then he looked down at the fireball and grinned. "Not to worry, Zac," he said. "It's only a bit of magic to help us see in the dark — it doesn't hurt."

"Oh, right," Zac muttered.

Cornelius coughed quietly to indicate they should all pay attention. "Now that everyone is safe and well, I think we should get back to business."

"Of course," Granny replied. "Lead the way."

His eyes twinkling, the old man tipped his hat, stepped to one side, and opened his arms dramatically.

Now Zac realized they were in a huge cavern. Ahead, the floor fell away into a deep canyon. It was as if they were in the belly of the world.

"Is that where we're going?" he gulped, pointing toward the other side of the chasm.

"Yes, lad," Granny said.

"But how do we get across?" He was half dreading the answer.

Cornelius let out a bellow of a laugh and looked up. "Why, we follow the moonlight, of course!" he yelled, his voice echoing in the vast space.

As the echoes died away, Julius extinguished the

fireball with a casual wave of his hand. Immediately, blackness swallowed them. Zac staggered back a few paces. Then he saw it.

High above them was a crack in the immense arching roof of the cavern, and through it Zac could see the moon, bright in the night sky. A beam of crystal moonlight cut like a blade through the darkness, drawing a straight line from where they were standing, on the edge of the canyon, to the opposite side.

"The moonlight marks the path," said Granny. "As long as we follow the beam we'll be safe. Just don't look down."

Cornelius grinned widely. "Shall we?" he said, clapping his hands. "This is my favorite part!"

Then he stepped off the edge of the canyon.

Zac was about to shout out in horror when he realized that Cornelius had not fallen. He was, in fact, standing on what looked to be thin air.

"I don't . . . I can't . . . how?" Zac spluttered in disbelief.

"Don't think about it too much," said Julius. "It's best just to get on with it."

"It's all right," said Granny. "I'll go first. Stay close. Follow in my footsteps exactly."

Zac nodded stiffly.

"Good lad," said Granny, and she stepped from the ledge into nothingness.

Zac crept forward. The abyss yawned before him like the mouth of some massive, hungry creature. Granny beckoned to him.

"I — I don't know if I can," he said.

"Of course you can," said Granny. "You made it through the Gateway. You just have to believe in yourself."

And so, taking a deep breath and wondering whether it might be his last, Zac stepped from the edge.

He was still holding his breath when his feet touched down on something solid. He opened his eyes, which had been jammed shut so tightly he'd begun to see stars. Granny was standing right in front of him. He hadn't fallen! He flashed a smile at her.

"Well done! Now follow me!" she cried.

Feeling a little braver now, Zac shuffled along behind Granny, sticking carefully to her path. Walking on moonlight was like nothing he'd ever experienced. His feet sank slightly, and each step sounded a little different from the last. Like a lost tune, his footsteps rang out into the void. He was walking on music.

When Zac finally reached the ledge on the other side, a wave of relief washed over him. His legs were shaking terribly, and he had to fight off an almost over-whelming urge to kiss the ground.

Cornelius shook him by the hand. "Tremendous!" he beamed. "Truly tremendous! Now we just need Julius."

Zac looked behind him. He had to stop himself from laughing.

Julius was about halfway across the moonlit path. He was on his hands and knees, very possibly about to be overtaken by a snail.

"Come on, Julius!" Cornelius boomed. "Pick up the pace!"

"Better safe than sorry, Cornelius!" replied Julius, inching toward them. When he was close enough, Cornelius leaned over and yanked him rather painfully to safety by the waistband of his pants.

"Where to now?" asked Zac. There was a sheer wall of rock in front of them.

"Almost there," Cornelius said. He pushed against the rock and it began to crack open, revealing a gap just wide enough for them to squeeze through.

"You first," said Granny.

Zac smiled, and wriggled through the opening. On the other side the nighttime air was warm and sweet. Under a colossal moon, a whole world opened up before him.

What a sight it was!

He was standing on a shelf of red rock miles above the ground. Below, a waterfall tumbled for a sparkling eternity. A patchwork of fields, woodlands, and mountains reached to the horizon and beyond. A swooshing sound overhead made him look up. Two enormous winged creatures were flying above him, gracefully rolling and dipping in the warm currents of air, their scales glittering so brightly they might have been carved from crystal. Zac watched them swoop out of sight.

"Dragons!" he breathed.

Footsteps behind told him that Granny and the others had arrived, too.

"It's amazing," he said. "It's stupendous . . . It's . . ."

Granny's eyes twinkled. She walked past Zac and stood on the very edge of the cliff, inhaling deeply. A wide smile broke over her wrinkled face.

"We're home, Zac," she said. "Welcome to Nocturne."

Rumpous Tinn flinched.

His skull was pounding with white-hot pain. He tried to touch the wound on his head, but found his hands were bound tightly.

He wasn't in his beautiful cell anymore. He had been tied to an uncomfortable iron chair in the center of a bare, circular room, with only one apparent exit. The walls were completely covered by blood-splashed mirrors, and torches cast flickering spotlights over his exhausted body.

Tinn's attention turned to the door. It opened to reveal the tall, elegant figure of a woman dressed completely in black. Her black cloak was so long it trailed on the floor, and a black skull mask, encrusted with glittering black jet, covered her entire head. Her eyes were hidden behind two circles of dark glass.

She stood before him for a long moment, and he felt her eyes bore into him from behind those eerie black lenses.

"Who are you?" asked Tinn.

"Mr. Tinn," she replied, bowing mockingly. "What a great pleasure this is." Her voice was a grating, metallic whisper that made him grit his teeth. Listening to her was as comfortable as chewing on tinfoil.

"My name is Shadow," she said, "leader of the Dream Stealers."

"Why have you brought me here?" Tinn demanded.

Shadow circled Tinn slowly, only speaking when she was standing in front of him again.

"Come now, Mr. Tinn. There is more to you than the frail old man who sits before me now. I know who you truly are."

"Oh, really? So, who am I?" said Tinn.

Shadow bent down, her glass eyes almost touching Tinn's face. "You are the Grandmaster of the Knights of Nod," she said.

Tinn looked into the blank face before him, his gaze steady. "The Knights disbanded years ago, after the last war," he lied. "They no longer exist in anything but history and myth. Everyone knows that."

"Do not mistake me for a fool," spat Shadow. "The Knights live on, in secret. Do not attempt to deny it."

"What do you want?" asked Tinn.

"Many years ago, you were visited by an oracle," said Shadow. "The story is legend among Dream Stealers. You were told that only three people could stop our rise to ultimate power. I believe you call them the Trinity."

Tinn stared, unflinching, into the circles of black.

"As you can imagine, I'd very much like to make sure that these three people are exterminated before they can become a problem."

"And you expect me to help?" said Tinn.

"My dear Mr. Tinn," said Shadow softly, "all I want is for you to tell me who they are."

Tinn laughed. "You must be mad."

"On the contrary," said Shadow, "my mind is clearer than ever. I must locate and destroy the Trinity. Tell me what you know now and you will not suffer, Mr. Tinn."

"You really want to choose this road?" said Tinn. "You genuinely believe that gaining more power is worth torturing Wakelings and poisoning Nocturne?"

"My destiny is to lead the Dream Stealers to victory!" Shadow boomed. "The more the Wakelings are shaken, the more power we can extract from their fear. Dark magic, as you call it, is the key to our future.

We shall take control. It is inevitable."

"And what will become of the rest of Nocturne?"

Shadow straightened up. "I am a reasonable person," she said. "Everyone in Nocturne will be given the chance to embrace the Dream Stealer way of life. Those too shortsighted to see the potential—"

"—will be killed?" said Tinn. "Adapt or die? Is that it?"

"That is how life has always been, Mr. Tinn," said Shadow. "No more of this. You will answer my question. Who are the Trinity?"

"I don't know," Tinn said defiantly.

"If you will not tell me, perhaps there is some other way I can track them down, some instrument that will lead me to them. Might you know about that?"

"I can't imagine what you're talking about," said Tinn.

"I see." Shadow paused. "In that case, you leave me no choice."

"Do what you must," Tinn whispered.

As Shadow's glass eyes delved deep into his mind, Tinn began to sweat. Flashes of long-forgotten memories began to play in his head like a slideshow, and he knew Shadow could see them, too. She was browsing through his mind like a catalog.

One image burned brighter in Tinn's mind than all the others.

Shadow was suddenly still. "Yes," she breathed. "That will do nicely."

She raised a black gloved hand.

A billow of smoke began to form around Tinn.

His head snapped back in shock. Eyes wide, sweat poured down his face. Wildly, he tried to shake off the horrifying vision that was forming in front of him. His eyes rolled back in their sockets.

"No . . . no, it can't be . . ."

Shadow flung her hands in the air, as if she were conducting a symphony of pain.

"She's dead! She's dead!" wailed Tinn. "Oh, Aris . . . my poor Aris, my sister . . ."

Rumpous Tinn's worst nightmare was engulfing him.

On the other side of the door, huddled in the darkness, was a girl. She was caked in grime, and her clothes were matted and torn.

Trembling, she listened to Tinn's screams.

Over the years she'd heard that sound many times, but it never ceased to frighten her. The Dream Stealers would come and go from this secret place. Creatures were herded here and hoarded — used as toys and for dark magic experiments. Humans, trolls, goblins, whatever the Dream Stealers could find. Most didn't last long.

Footsteps echoed along the corridor.

The girl pressed herself flat against the rock wall and made herself invisible as two Dream Stealers turned the corner, their black cloaks flowing, their silver-encased arms folded across their chests. One of them glanced at the spot where the girl stood clutching her heart, but saw nothing. A moment later they were gone.

The girl reappeared. The old man was alone in there, and for some reason she wanted to help him. But she had to be careful.

There was quiet for the briefest of moments, then the cries of Rumpous Tinn shattered the silence again.

8

Roughly cut stairs in the rock led Zac and the others down the face of the cliff.

At the bottom, Julius's fireball burned brighter, illuminating a hidden cove behind the thundering waterfall.

"Ahoy there!"

The voice came from a chubby rowboat bobbing about in the cove. Inside it, a figure so tall and thin he looked like a drawing of a stickman was waving frantically at them, as if they might not spot him. He was wearing a tattered top hat and tails, and his clothes were far too short for his gangly arms and legs. The boat was rocking wildly.

The stickman clicked his long fingers and the oars

began to move of their own accord, propelling him suddenly toward the shore and knocking him off his feet. When he reached shallow water, he leapt from the boat and came splashing excitedly toward them.

"Cornelius! Julius! You're late. Where's Tinn?"

"He's been taken," said Cornelius. "We were ambushed in the Eternal Forest. Dream Stealers, I think."

A look of horror crawled over the stickman's face. His mouth moved, but no words came out. He swayed a little, and Zac thought he looked like a skinny tree about to crash to the ground.

"But all is not lost," continued Cornelius. "Tinn distracted the Dream Stealers long enough for Julius and I to slip away and reach Eve Wonder. As you can see, she's agreed to return home with us, and she's brought along her grandson, Zac."

The man held out a very long, lean hand. "By the stars," he said, "Eve Wonder. I've heard all about you. It's a great pleasure to meet you at last. My name is Gideon Small. I'm a Knight of Nod, too."

"Yes, yes, let's get moving, shall we?" said Cornelius, fidgeting with his mustache. "There isn't a moment to spare. Our first order of business is obvious. We must plan how to rescue Tinn, so we need to get to Slumber City as quickly as possible. That's the capital of Nocturne," he added, for Zac's benefit.

They waded out to the boat and climbed aboard. Gideon sat at the front, facing everyone else. When they were all settled, he clicked his fingers, and the magic oars began to swish through the water.

"But we're heading straight for the waterfall," said Zac.

Gideon smiled. "Of course we are, dear boy. Going through is so much quicker than going around."

Before Zac could think about the wisdom of this, they had reached the roaring wall of water. Burying his head in his knees, he waited to be crushed. Nothing happened. It was as if an enormous invisible umbrella was protecting them. He sat up when he heard the others chuckling. Soon the waters gave way to a wide river, and the conversation turned back to Tinn's predicament.

"If the Dream Stealers have him, there's no telling where he might be," said Julius. "But if it was one of their evil crews of werewolves or vampires that made the snatch, we'd have a fair idea where to start. That's the trouble with Dream Stealers. Under those masks, they're people just like us, humans who have turned to the dark side. Without their disguises, they blend in, so we're never sure where our enemies are."

As they sped on across the water, Zac noticed twinkling in the darkness up ahead. The lights drew nearer, and a shape emerged from the gloom. Zac blinked.

"Granny."

"Yes, lad?"

"Is that a double-decker bus floating toward us?"

"Oh, that'll be a leftover from some Wakeling's dream," said Granny with a smile. "It would amaze you what turns up. Some people have the strangest imaginations! You know, there are merchants who make a living out of venturing into the Dream Plains and salvaging all sorts of things to sell."

"But it's a bus! Buses don't float!"

"Well, that one does," said Granny.

The rusty red bus bobbed gently past. There were round paddles where the wheels should have been. A tiny old man waved happily from the driver's seat. Zac lost sight of it as the rowboat rounded a bend in the river.

"Look up ahead!" said Granny suddenly. "Slumber City!"

The river broadened and an island came into view. A great mountain rose up into the night sky, twinkling with countless lights. It reminded Zac of a giant Christmas tree. A huge outer wall encircled the city. It was made with enormous stones, each one the size of a car. Zach wondered who could possibly have built such a thing.

"The greatest city in all of Nocturne," said Cornelius proudly. "And the highest peak — Slumber Mountain."

Gideon rolled his eyes. "Do excuse Cornelius, Zac," he said breezily. "He's such a big softy."

Cornelius's face reddened, and laughter rocked the boat as it glided into the shadow of the city. They swept up to a set of immense metal doors under a tangled curtain of seaweed, drawing level with a little platform on which sat an oversized wooden hut.

"Sshh! The guard has to let us in," said Cornelius.

"Guard?"

The door of the hut creaked open, and something appeared, silhouetted against the cozy glow from inside. Whatever the creature was, it was too big for the hut; it seemed to be struggling to get out.

"What's that?" whispered Zac.

"A troll," said Granny softly.

The creature took a deep breath and, an instant later, came crashing out.

Zac gasped. The troll was gigantic — twice as tall as a man — and as wide as the bus that had just floated past. It wore a massive metal helmet and mesh chest armor over its leathery body. The troll stood for a moment examining the boat, its head to one side. Zac swallowed as he felt its gaze pass over him.

The troll belched. "What's your business?" it growled in a voice so deep that Zac's ears began to ring.

Gideon beamed as he hopped up on to the platform.

Tall and gangly though he was, even he was dwarfed by the height of the troll, whose meaty hands were bigger than Gideon's entire head.

"Oh, just returning from a trip to Port Town," he said cheerily. He pointed toward Zac and the others. "Thought I'd take the family along."

The troll stared at the odd group in the boat. Gideon gave them all a little wink. He seemed to be enjoying himself, but Zac had never been so nervous. At last, the troll grunted, and shrugged its great shoulders.

"Very well," it said. "Go ahead."

Gideon bowed and hopped back into the boat.

The troll lifted a huge ivory horn on a rope around its neck and placed it to its mouth. When it blew, the racket was as loud as a ship's foghorn. Seconds later another horn sounded from the other side of the wall, and the gates rumbled open. The boat shook and the dark water churned.

"Take us in," said Gideon, with a wave of his hand. Once again the oars jolted into action, steering the boat into the city.

A little port opened up before them, filled with vessels of every description. There were fishing boats like those in the Waking World. But Zac could also see a whole range of more unusual crafts: a pirate ship made of bones; a trawler carved from an iceberg that didn't seem to be melting; and what looked very much like an extra-large coconut shell with a sail. An old sea dog even drifted past them in a tin bathtub, sleeping peacefully under an umbrella.

Beyond the water were the docks, and beyond the docks were rows of tumbledown houses and narrow cobbled streets that wound out of sight. Slumber Mountain rose spectacularly above the port. Now that he could see it more clearly, Zac realized every square foot of cliff had been built on. There were towers, quaint cottages, and crooked buildings with haphazard extensions jutting out at all sorts of angles. One building had three extra floors balanced on top of it like a house of cards, and another had a windmill sticking out of the roof.

When the boat reached the buzzing quayside, Zac and the Knights climbed up the steps to the harbor walkway, avoiding the slithering seaweed.

Had Zac been anywhere else, he might have felt conspicuous walking around in his pajamas and bathrobe, but some of the people here were dressed so strangely it didn't seem to matter. It was as if Slumber City's residents had taken bits of style from every time period in the Waking World and mashed them all together. One man walked past wearing a bowler hat, a string vest, and a pair of orange velvet flared pants. Another wore yellow shorts with a tartan T-shirt and pink gloves. There were also lots of hats — beanies, bonnets, and berets, even a few piled high with fruit or flowers. One woman seemed to have a real bird's nest in hers.

"Come on," said Granny. "We must get to The Forty Winks and formulate a plan."

"The Forty Winks?" asked Zac, watching a man cycle past on a penny-farthing bike that was belching smoke.

Granny glanced around to make sure no one was eavesdropping. "It's the secret headquarters of the Order," she whispered. "A pub on the other side of the city."

"Your secret headquarters is a *pub*?" said Zac. "And the Dream Stealers have never found it?"

Granny smiled. "This is no ordinary pub."

"It's protected by powerful magic," said Gideon. "A Knight cannot reveal the location of The Forty Winks to anyone who's not connected to the Order. As far as I can tell the spell is unbreakable."

They made their way through a labyrinth of torch-lit streets and twisting alleyways. Zac read some of the shop names as they hurried past: MADAME MORTIMER'S MASSIVE MUSHROOMS; WILBUR J. CRINKLESNITCH & SON APOTHECARY — RARE PIXIE DUST IN STOCK; WILLOW THE WARLOCK'S WITCH AND WIZARD SECOND-HAND EMPORIUM. There seemed to be at least one pub on every street, and most were filled with a rabble of cheery customers.

Zac lost count of how many corners they turned before they ventured up a winding cobbled lane. A minute or two later, Cornelius stopped in his tracks and turned to his companions.

They were standing in front of a row of run-down buildings, and sandwiched between two of them was a crumbling cake of a tavern. The windows were completely black with grime. A crooked sign hung above the door. It was so faded that the gold letters were barely visible: THE FORTY WINKS.

"*This* is it?" said Zac. "This is your HQ?"

"Yes," replied Cornelius, looking a little hurt.

"I mean it's, um, brilliant," Zac said quickly.

Cornelius cheered up at once. He walked up to the prehistoric door and placed his hand on the doorknob, which was shaped like a crescent moon.

"Well," he said with a wink, "shall we?"

9

Fresh, cold water trickled down Rumpous Tinn's face, waking him from an exhausted slumber. His dry eyes cracked open. The first thing he saw was a wet rag floating gently above his head.

"Who's there?" he said.

The rag dropped to the floor.

"A friend."

Tinn recognized the voice. It belonged to the invisible person he'd heard earlier.

"You're weak," she said. "You ought to eat."

Glancing around, Tinn realized he was back in his cell. He must have lost consciousness. The things Shadow had made him see . . . But he'd managed to resist telling her anything. He shook the horror from his head. His mind ached.

A plate of bacon and eggs lay on the floor beside him. He was so hungry he didn't even care if it was poisoned. Grabbing the plate, he began to eat greedily.

"Drink," said the little voice once again, and a sumptuous goblet was pushed into Tinn's hands. He took a long draft. The water rushed through his body, immediately rousing every muscle and nerve. He sat back against the wall and let out a sigh.

"Thank you," he said.

"That's all right," said the voice.

"I must confess," added Tinn, "that I am very curious to meet you properly. What is your name?"

"My name?"

There was silence for a moment.

"It's Noelle," said the voice softly. "My name's Noelle."

"A beautiful name. Mine is Rumpous Tinn."

"I like my name," said Noelle. "My mum used to sing a song about it. It's been so long since I've heard anyone use it."

Tinn leaned forward, searching the room for any sign of movement.

"Tell me, Noelle," he murmured, "how did you come to be in this place?"

"It was so long ago," whispered Noelle. "I can only

remember flashes of what happened. Our village was attacked one night. The screams woke me up. My mum sang to me. She was tryin' to keep me quiet."

"Who attacked your village, Noelle?"

"Vampires. It was vampires, Mr. Tinn. Sent by the Dream Stealers to drive us out. They were feedin' on almost everyone they could find, but they kept some of us alive so they could bring us here, to this place. They have a deal with the Dream Stealers, see. The vampires bring folk to the Dream Stealers, and the Dream Stealers keep them here in secret and practice their dark magic on 'em."

Tinn sighed.

"Mum and me hid as best we could, but they smelt us out us eventually. Mum wouldn't let me go. I was screamin', so they bit her. And she fell."

Tinn bowed his head.

"I was brought here with a few of us from my village. They're all gone now. The Dream Stealers finished 'em off."

"But they didn't finish you, did they?" he said softly. "You were different from the others. You could disappear."

Tinn saw the air flutter slightly, and out of nothingness a girl emerged. She was pretty with dark, soft features and olive skin, and she was dressed in rags. She was crying.

"At first . . . ," she said, wiping her hazel eyes,

"at first I couldn't control it—it just happened. I'd disappear sometimes when I was scared. But as I got older and stronger, I started understandin' it. Now I can be invisible whenever I choose. That's how I survived down here for so long. When I'm invisible I can go wherever I please. I steal food—they got kitchens here. Some of them Dream Stealers stay for days at a time. And they have to feed their prisoners—gotta keep 'em alive for a while at least. I nicked your breakfast off the kitchen table."

"And most delicious it was, too." Tinn smiled. "Noelle, I have a question. If you can slip past doors and such, why have you never escaped?"

She laughed. "You think I ain't tried? I can only get so far, up to the ground level. But the exit is guarded."

"Well"—Tinn smiled again—"with my help, I'm sure we can get past a few guards."

"You don't understand," she said. "It ain't guarded by Dream Stealers, by people. It's guarded by water—by a lake. The water is . . . it's alive. It's bewitched. Anyone who touches it is pulled into a watery grave, sucked into the lake and drowned. I'm too scared to swim. I've seen it happen."

Tinn's face darkened. "Why didn't I know about this place?" he muttered quietly to himself.

"They built it in secret," said Noelle, "a long time ago. I've heard the Dream Stealers talkin'. In the old days lots of 'em were rich and they wanted a comfortable place somewhere out of the way where they could come to practice their dark stuff. So they built this place up here in the North. Nobody knows about it, except the goblins, and they only sneak in and steal food, or prisoners. It ain't possible to escape."

"Nothing is impossible," said Tinn. "There's always a way."

Noelle rolled her eyes doubtfully.

"I have a question for you, Noelle," said Tinn. "Have you ever heard of the Knights of Nod?"

"Yeah, I have," she said. "I've heard prisoners telling stories about the Knights. Some of them said they died out after the last war. Other people said they never existed to begin with. They were just a fairy tale made up to make people feel safer."

"And what do you think?" Tinn asked.

Noelle pursed her lips in thought, then said, "Well, I think they're probably a fairy tale, too."

Tinn smiled sadly to himself.

"What?" asked Noelle. "What you smilin' at?"

"Oh, my dear girl," replied Tinn, holding his hands up, "I am certainly not laughing *at* you. It's just that I find it a little sad that all this time you believed the Knights of Nod to be nothing more than a bedtime story when here you are, talking to their leader."

10

Zac and the others shuffled into The Forty Winks out of the cold night air, and were greeted by the warm, inviting glow of candlelight. The room in front of them was long and narrow, and divided into padded booths furnished with chunky tables and mismatched chairs and benches. The wooden floor looked ancient and rather sticky. The bar was at the far end.

As they trooped forward, a man's head popped up from behind the counter. He had a bushy black mustache and a few wispy strands of hair on his head, and his many chins wobbled as he moved.

"Who's that?!" he yelled.

"Relax, old man." Cornelius grinned. "It's us."

"Oh, Cornelius!" said the head. "Thank the stars you're all right!"

The man struggled to his feet. He had very little neck and was wearing a puffy checked shirt under a plum velvet vest. His mouth fell open when he saw Granny.

"E-Eve?" he stammered. "Eve Wonder? Is that you?"

Granny stepped forward. "How are you, Barnaby?"

"By the stars!" he yelled, and rushed over to greet her. "Eve Wonder!" He hugged her tightly. "I can't believe it. For so long we all thought you were . . ."

"Dead?"

"Well, yes. You've been gone for fifty years, Eve! And then the Dream Stealers returned, and Tinn decided to tell us the truth — that you'd been hidden in the Waking World, and he was going to bring you back."

"Well," replied Granny, "here I am."

"And the Dream Stealers won't know what's hit 'em!" said Barnaby. "But where is Tinn?"

"Come," said Granny. "I think we should all sit down."

"Good idea. I'll fetch some powder-keg punch," said Barnaby.

They sat in one of the booths and Barnaby brought a tray full of drinks. Zac lifted a heavy tankard and took a swig of the clear liquid inside. It was wonderfully cold and sweet, and when it hit his stomach, he felt heat burst through his entire body. He gulped the rest gratefully.

"Well?" said Barnaby. "What's happened?"

Cornelius began to recount the evening's events, from Tinn's capture in the Eternal Forest, to escaping through the Gateway, to finding Granny waiting there with her grandson.

"Seems a bit fishy that the Dream Stealers knew where to find Tinn," said Barnaby. "I wonder if they've been following one of us?"

"It's possible," said Cornelius.

Barnaby turned to Zac, who became very aware that all eyes were now on him.

"Pleased to meet you, Zac," he said, reaching a fat hand over the table. "My name is Barnaby Smudge and I am the chief watchman of The Forty Winks." He puffed out his chest proudly, and because there was a lot of Barnaby to puff out, several candles were knocked over.

"Pleased to meet you," said Zac, shaking Barnaby's hand. The bartender's fingers were like thick sausages.

"No one gets into HQ without going through Barnaby first," said Julius.

"And speaking of HQ," said Gideon, "shouldn't we be heading there now? We must decide what should be done."

"Right you are," replied Cornelius. "Barnaby, take us down, will you?"

"Of course." Barnaby toddled back to the bar. "Is

everyone ready?" he shouted. Then he reached over and pulled on one of the large beer taps.

There was a loud *clunk-clank-clunk*, and the floorboards beneath Zac's feet disappeared. He looked wildly at Granny.

"Hold on to your hat," she said.

The bench in the booth tipped forward, dropping them down through a black hole in the floor.

Zac found himself sliding down a chute so fast he thought his stomach might bump into his brain. He could hear the others thundering along beside him.

"Wheeeeeeeeeheeeeheeee!"

That was Gideon.

Before he knew what had happened, Zac *whooshed* out of the darkness and landed with a bounce on a soft, springy surface. The floor was a trampoline. They had arrived in a large circular room, brightly decorated in red and gold. There were two heavy wooden doors on opposite sides.

"What now?" he said.

"Follow me," said Cornelius. He half walked, half bounced to one of the doors, and pulled it open to reveal a grand corridor.

Cornelius led the way along the corridor and through a set of double doors to a remarkable room.

A gold spiral staircase wound up toward the high

ceiling, which was painted with a picture of the night sky. In the very center of the picture, a moon actually glowed. A tall window provided a panoramic view over the city and beyond. Every square inch of the walls was covered with books, and there were several ladders on rails attached to the shelves. The room was alive with the sound of ticking, clicking, whirring, and buzzing from intricate devices stacked everywhere. Some devices had been taken apart; others seemed to be in the process of reassembling themselves. Scrolls and parchments were scattered everywhere, and a miniature steam train sped happily around the room.

"Right," said Cornelius. "Everyone here? Good, good."

"Where exactly is 'here'?" inquired Zac.

"Grandmaster's quarters," said Granny.

"But we're deep underground!" said Zac. "How can there be a window in here with a view?"

Granny grinned. Zac got the feeling that he wouldn't understand even if she told him.

"Grandad!"

A boy and girl around Zac's age came rushing down the spiral staircase. They leapt the final few steps and threw themselves at Cornelius.

"What took you so long, Grandad?" asked the boy, excitedly.

"He won't tell you, squirt," replied the girl, rolling her eyes.

"Tilly, Tom, there are some people I'd like you to meet," said Cornelius. He turned to Granny. "Evegenia Wonder," he continued, "it's my great pleasure to introduce you to my grandchildren, Tilly and Tom Huggins."

Tom and Tilly stared at Granny.

"Is this the lady you told us about, Grandad?" said Tilly.

"The one you thought was dead?" added Tom.

"Pleased to meet you," said Granny.

"Hello," said Tilly. She was tall and skinny, and her messy blond hair fell over her face as she smiled at Granny. She had a gap between her front teeth.

"How d'you do?" said Tom. He was much shorter than his sister, with unruly short black hair, a freckled face, and thick eyebrows.

"And this is Eve's grandson, Zac."

Tilly and Tom sized him up. Zac stiffened. Whenever he met anyone his own age, the outcome was usually miserable.

"All right?" said Tom and Tilly.

"All right?" replied Zac, nodding slightly.

"Jolly good, jolly good!" Cornelius beamed. "Children, you stay here and chat. Get to know each other and whatnot. We'll head upstairs. Tilly, are your parents up there?"

"Yes, Grandad."

With that, the Knights of Nod began climbing the golden spiral staircase. Granny squeezed Zac's shoulder as she went by.

"We won't be long, lad," she said.

When they were out of sight, Tom slapped his hand on his forehead. "That always happens," he said.

"What does?" asked Zac.

"They always go off and leave us just as things get interesting."

"They're hardly going to tell you everything, Tom, are they?" said his sister.

"Why not?" replied Tom, looking miffed. "I'm a Knight, too, aren't I?"

"You are?" said Zac, surprised.

"Well, kind of," said Tom, turning pink. "We've just started our training."

"Yeah," said Tilly. "Last month. Grandad was thrilled to bits when Mum and Dad gave permission. He'd been telling them for ages that our magic should be developed. Most people simply don't bother anymore. It's easy not to in a place like Nocturne."

"It was the proudest moment of his life," added Tom.

"He was crying and everything." He looked at Zac and raised an eyebrow. "What about you?"

"Me?"

"Yeah," said Tom. "With your granny being such an important Knight, you must have some powers, too, right?"

"Well, I — I don't know," said Zac timidly. "I — I don't think so. I'm not from here, you see."

Tilly's brow furrowed. "What do you mean?"

Zac swallowed hard. They didn't know. They didn't know that he was from another world, that he was an alien. When they found out they certainly wouldn't want anything to do with him. Things here would be just like they were back home. He didn't belong *anywhere*. He found himself backing away. Before he knew it, he was pressed against a huge bookcase.

"That's the thing, you see," he said. "I'm not from Nocturne at all. I'm from the Waking World."

This time Tilly and Tom stepped back, their eyes as wide as full moons.

"You mean, you're a Wakeling?" whispered Tom.

"'Fraid so," said Zac with a sigh. "Well, part of me is. Granny was born here, so I suppose part of me is from here, too. I suppose I'm a bit of both."

Tom's mouth fell open. "Brilliant!" he said.

"Unbelievable," croaked Tilly.

They both gazed at Zac in the way someone might look at the most interesting animal at the zoo.

"What?" said Zac. "What is it?"

"Sorry," whispered Tom. "It's just that we've never met anyone from the Waking World before. What's it like there? And how come you're wearing pajamas? Does everyone there dress like that all the time?"

Zac had forgotten about his pajamas. He blushed, tying the belt on his robe a little tighter.

"Oh . . . this is just what I wear to bed," he babbled. "Usually I wear different stuff." He fought back a smirk. "Sort of like what you have on, actually."

Tom was wearing terrible bright blue pants, with a pink shirt and vest.

There was a moment's silence. Zac put his hands in his pockets and felt something cold and metallic. He jingled it between his fingers.

"What have you got there?" quizzed Tilly.

Zac pulled his hand out and opened it. Nestling in his palm were two shiny ten-pence pieces.

"What are those?" said Tom excitedly.

"Coins," replied Zac. He held out his hand. "Here," he said. "Now you can say you've got something from the Waking World."

Tilly and Tom slowly took the coins from Zac's hand.

"Thanks," said Tom.

"What are they used for?" asked Tilly.

"Coins are money," said Zac. "If you want to buy something from someone, you give them some of these and they give you something in return."

"We know what money is," Tom said with a laugh.

"Yeah," added Tilly. "But it's a bit strange that people should use lumps of metal. We use teeth."

"Teeth?"

"Yeah, look," said Tilly. She pulled a little leather pouch from her pocket and opened it to reveal a pile of teeth. "These were collected by the tooth fairy from under the pillows of sleeping children in the Waking World. That's what we use as money here."

Zac almost choked.

"They've been cleaned, you know," she added, noticing his disgusted expression.

"Did you . . . did you say the tooth fairy?" Zac stammered.

"Yeah," said Tom, still examining his coin. "Surely you've heard of her?"

"Of course I have," said Zac. "It's just that she's make-believe."

"Make-believe?" said Tom.

"Yeah," muttered Zac. "I mean, most children my age think the tooth fairy is a story for babies."

Tom stared at Zac for a second and then looked at his sister. "Completely bonkers," he said, pointing to his head. "Hey, you want us to show you around?"

"I'm supposed to stay here," said Zac.

"Not now! Later, when everyone's asleep."

"We know HQ inside out," added Tilly.

Zac only thought about it for a second. This place did seem pretty cool. And he'd just met two kids who didn't think he was a freak. He wasn't going to blow it now.

"OK," he said. "If you're sure."

"Only, don't tell anyone," warned Tom. "We're not supposed to. There's all sorts of weird stuff lying around. An old shoe attacked me last week . . ."

At that moment, Granny and the others reappeared.

Tom nudged Zac in the ribs. "Remember," he whispered, "don't say anything."

"Right," said Zac, wondering what sort of surprises lay ahead.

11

The dining room of the Knights' headquarters was oval with a polished floor and a round table, on which places had been set for everyone.

Here, Zac was introduced to Tilly and Tom's parents, Humphrey and Holly Huggins, who ran HQ.

"How do you do!" Humphrey beamed as he shook hands with Granny and Zac. "Such a pleasure!"

He was a neat man, tall and lean with sleek, jet-black hair, piercing blue eyes, and a pencil mustache. He didn't so much talk as fire words like a machine gun.

"So pleased to meet you, dears," said Holly Huggins. She was short and plump with curly blond hair and a round face. Her voice was gentle. "Please do make yourselves at home."

Mr. and Mrs. Huggins had prepared a feast. Zac's mouth watered. There was hot broth, crusty bread spread thickly with golden butter, cheese, fat sausages, and a large cauldron of melted chocolate in which they could dip fresh fruit and giant marshmallows.

Zac ate until he could barely move.

"Hey, Zac," said Tom through a mouthful of sausage, "tell us about the Waking World. What's it like?"

"Yeah," said Tilly. "Is it anything like here?"

"A little, I suppose," said Zac, tugging nervously at the belt of his robe. It felt strange to be the center of attention. "It's actually a bit dull compared to what I've seen of Nocturne so far. In the Waking World, things just do what they're supposed to. There aren't any dragons, or floating buses, or magical rowboats . . ."

Tom looked disappointed.

"No magic?" asked Tilly

"It's a different sort of magic," said Zac. "Like television."

"Telewhat?" said Tom, furrowing his eyebrows.

"Television. It's a little box that shows moving picture stories. Watching television is how most people in the Waking World spend their spare time."

"What, they just stare at it?"

"I heard about one of those!" said Tilly. "A merchant is supposed to have found one in the Dream Plains. He brought it out and switched it on and sure enough, there were the moving pictures. It was fine for a while, but then one night, he got sucked in! He was trapped. Then the telly-viser thingy went mad. It ran around, sucking people into different stories. It took twenty people to capture it. They tried and tried, but they never could get those people back out."

"That's terrible!" said Zac. "But in the Waking World, televisions never go around sucking people in. Not in that way. They just sort of sit there."

"Why bother to have one, then?" said Tom.

"Zac," said Granny over the chatter, "Holly has volunteered to take you up to the city tomorrow to get you some new clothes. Isn't that kind?"

Zac looked down at his pajamas. He nodded with relief at Mrs. Huggins. "Thanks," he said.

"No trouble, dear," she answered cheerily. "I need to collect something anyway." She glanced carefully at the other Knights.

"Can we come, too, Mum?" asked Tom.

"Yeah," pleaded Tilly. "Can we? Please?"

Mrs. Huggins rolled her eyes. "All right," she sighed to her children. "But no fighting and no sneaking off, understand?"

"Yes, Mum," they chimed.

"What will you be doing, Granny?" asked Zac, dipping another marshmallow.

"Well, lad," said Granny, "I'll be preparing with the others."

"For what?"

"The search to find Rumpous Tinn."

"Can't I go with you?" he asked.

"Yeah!" cried Tom. "Me, too!"

"And me!" said Tilly.

"This is no job for children," Cornelius concluded firmly.

"Right," said Mrs. Huggins, before they could argue further. "Come on, bedtime. Zac, you can share with Tom. I've already prepared a bed."

"Nice one!" said Tom. "Come on, Zac, I'll show you my room."

They said good night to the others, and Zac followed Tom down the gaudy red and gold corridor, wondering what on earth a bedroom in Nocturne might look like.

"Do you actually live in this place, then?" he said.

"Not usually," said Tom. "We have a house above The Forty Winks. Knights usually have a home somewhere outside HQ. Mum and Dad own the pub. It's been passed down on my mum's side for generations. Her family have always been sort of honorary Knights. That's how she met my dad. Grandad brought him to the pub and they fell in love. Disgusting, really. Here we are."

Tom's room was wide and spacious, although just about every inch of the floor was covered in clothes, books, and colorful parchments. The walls were plastered with posters depicting fantastic creatures.

"That's yours," said Tom, pointing to a comfortable-looking bed in the corner.

"This is great," said Zac. He leapt onto the bed, sinking into the fluffy duvet.

Tom jumped onto his bed, too. "Just wait until you see the rest of this place," he said, waving his arms, but shut up as Mrs. Huggins popped her head around the door.

"Get to bed now, boys! We're up early tomorrow. And don't stand on that mattress, Thomas. I've told you before. Good night, Zac." She left the door open just enough for a little torchlight to dance into the room.

"We'll have a couple of hours' sleep," said Tom as they climbed into bed. "Then we'll get up and meet Tilly, and we can show you around."

"All right," said Zac, yawning. "See you in a bit."

Within seconds, Tom was snoring loudly, while Zac tossed and turned. Eventually, he got out of bed and began browsing through the books and papers on the floor. A parchment magazine called *Myth and Magic* caught his attention. He picked it up and stared at the cover. A menacing face with huge teeth sneered at him. Zac read the headline:

MONSTROUS SPECIAL EDITION
THE MOST DANGEROUS CREATURES IN THE DREAM PLAINS. BE PREPARED OR BE LUNCH!

Zac flipped through the pages. The magazine was crammed full of illustrated articles about the most terrible monsters in Nocturne: goblins, ghouls, mountain trolls, chimeras, and many others. It seemed that most of these monsters had walked straight out of the dreams — or nightmares — of Wakelings, and set up home in dark corners of Nocturne.

"Just a bit of light reading, eh, Tom?" he murmured to himself.

He flipped another page and saw the foul creature from the front cover, then began to read:

The werewolf is one of the most feared monsters in all of Nocturne. Werewolves are known for their ability to blend in among humans, and for their lust for blood. A werewolf will always play with its food. A common misconception is that werewolves only transform during a full moon. This is untrue. They can transform at any time they wish. In *Myth and Magic's*

"Most Terrifying Ways to Die" poll last year, Werewolf Attack finished third—behind only Vampire Bite and Dream Stealer Assault.

> Danger Level: extreme
> Size: huge in werewolf form
> Speed: don't even try to run
> Weaponry: teeth, strength, guile . . . pretty much everything
> Best Defense: silver
> Likely Outcome: death—or, if you're lucky, transformation into a werewolf

A door slammed in the corridor. Zac jumped. He stared out into the passageway through the tiny gap in the open door. Nobody seemed to be there. He laughed at himself for feeling startled in a place as safe as the HQ of the Knights of Nod. His eyelids were beginning to feel heavy, and he suddenly realized how exhausted he was. He tossed *Myth and Magic* back on the floor, then climbed into bed and drifted off to sleep with images of monsters swimming in his head.

12

Tinn paced his cell stroking his beard, the cogs in his brain whizzing and clicking at full speed.

A swooshing sound broke his concentration, and he stopped dead.

"Noelle? Is that you?"

The air fluttered. Noelle appeared before him, smiling.

"I got it," she said, dangling a large rusty key.

"Bravo, dear girl," said Tinn. "And how does it look out there?"

"The corridor outside is guarded," Noelle said. "But the rest of the place seems quiet. It's nighttime. Most of the Dream Stealers who were here have gone to plunder the Dream Plains."

"What about guards?"

"Five Dream Stealers," replied Noelle.

"That's not so bad," said Tinn, with the hint of a smile. He stood up and stretched like an athlete.

"And one mountain troll," added Noelle quickly.

Tinn froze mid-stretch and raised an eyebrow. "Mountain troll, you say?" He rubbed his head and sighed. "Oh, good."

Noelle bit her bottom lip.

"Well, we may as well get this over with," said Tinn. "You know what to do?"

"Yes."

"Good."

She was about to become invisible when Tinn put a gentle hand on her shoulder.

"After you have opened the door, your job is over. Do you understand?"

She nodded.

"There will be no heroics," he insisted. "You will stay hidden. Agreed?"

Noelle shrugged. "I swear," she said. And with that she disappeared.

Tinn crept over to the door and pressed his ear against

the cold silver surface. After a few seconds there was a faint click. He smiled and waved his hand. The heavy door swung open in silence. That part was easy.

The corridor beyond his cell was narrow and starkly lit, with a jagged rock ceiling. Tinn stood at the entrance for a moment, his eyes closed. He breathed deeply, gathering his magic. Then he filled his lungs, pushed up the sleeves of his robe, and walked forward.

The hard part was about to begin.

Rumpous Tinn's heart thundered in his ancient ears as he strode from his cell into the corridor.

A Dream Stealer was stationed across the passageway, standing to attention in his silver skull mask, his bone armor glinting. Then he spotted Tinn and his crossed arms dropped.

"He's escaped! He's out!" he yelled.

Instantly another two guards came running, shooting inky jets of foul dark magic from their outstretched arms. Tinn waved his hand, dispersing the jets, then stamped hard on the floor. The stone cracked, and a shockwave ripped through the air, throwing the guards across the corridor, where they fell limply to the ground.

"Look out!"

Noelle's cry came too late. Tinn was hit in the back with such force that he was thrown half the length of the passageway. He got up and wheeled around. Two more guards faced him, and behind them stood a monstrous mountain troll. As the troll roared, the two remaining Dream Stealers charged.

Tinn leapt into the air, flipping over the guards and shooting a spell at the troll's head. Before it reached the creature, the spell split in two and became a pair of tiny, colorful birds. They swooped and swirled in the air, distracting the flailing monster.

As the birds faded, Tinn fired another spell at the sidetracked guards, encasing them in a huge block of ice.

A deafening roar filled the hallway. He had the troll's attention again.

As Tinn spun he saw Noelle had made herself visible. She was bravely trying to draw the troll away from him.

"Noelle!" cried Tinn. "I warned you to stay clear!"

At that moment the furious troll grabbed the girl and hurled her across the corridor like a doll. She lay motionless on the dirty floor.

Tinn dropped to his knees, gasping for breath. He knew he didn't have much time. As fast as he could, he sent out thousands of twisting threads that wound around the troll's huge body. In an instant it was bound tight. It struggled for a moment, then fell with a crash that shook the corridor.

Exhausted, Tinn stumbled over to Noelle's unconscious body. He knelt beside her and felt for a pulse.

"Thank the stars," he muttered.

A crack from the block of ice told him the Dream Stealers would soon be free. He scooped the girl off the floor, heaved her over his shoulder, and made for the staircase.

13

Zac stood in a freezing black fog, shivering and afraid. He didn't have a clue where he was. He could barely see his hand in front of his face.

"Granny?" he said. "Tom? Hello?"

There was no reply.

He was suddenly aware of something in his palm. The blackness cleared a little and he was startled to realize that he was clutching a dagger with a sapphire-encrusted handle.

Footsteps came from nowhere. They were heavy, but whatever they belonged to was traveling at great speed. There was a growling gust of wind, and a monster tore out of the fog toward him.

Zac screamed and fell backward, clutching the dagger. The creature swooped. In that second, Zac held out the blade. There was a howl of pain, a flash, and the air was filled with smoldering ash. Just as suddenly as it had arrived, the creature was gone.

Zac stood up, his heart pumping. The darkness seemed to be closing in.

"Help!"

"Zac?"

"Help me!"

"Zac! Wake up!"

"Wha—?"

"Wake up!"

He was back in Tom's room, and Tom was standing over him, looking rather scared.

"Are you all right?" he said. "You were shouting and thrashing around."

"Oh . . . it was nothing . . . just a dream . . ."

"A dream?" said Tom, his eyes wide. "You had a dream?"

"Yeah. So?"

"People here don't dream, Zac."

"What?"

"People in Nocturne," said Tom. "We don't dream. We never have." He looked at Zac enviously. "What's it like to dream?"

"I dunno," Zac said. "It's just like real life, only anything can happen."

"What, anything?"

"Seems that way. You've really never had a dream, ever?"

Tom shook his head. "What did you dream about just then?" he said. "Was it a bad dream?"

The image of the creature flying toward him flashed in Zac's mind. He didn't want to think about it.

"I can't remember," he said, feeling a little guilty about lying. "Dreams sometimes leave you as soon as you wake up. They disappear like smoke. It happens all the time."

"Oh, right," said Tom, disappointed. "We'd better go. Tilly will be waiting."

Zac half climbed and half fell out of bed. Yawning widely, he threw on his robe and slippers, and followed Tom to the door. Tom peeked out into the corridor.

"All clear," he said, "Come on."

The dazzling colors of the grand corridor had been replaced by a ghostly blue glow. Zac shivered. They tiptoed along the passage until they reached a set of double doors.

"Tilly said she'd meet us here," said Tom. "She won't be long, she's never late."

As they waited, Zac's eyes were drawn to the portraits that hung on the walls in majestic golden frames. The people in the paintings stared down at them, almost as if they knew that they were up to no good.

Suddenly there was an icy-cold hand on the back of his neck. He yelped.

It was Tilly. She giggled at the look of fright on his face. Tom was trying his best not to laugh. Zac was glad the corridor was dark, because he felt himself turning a magnificent shade of red.

"Sorry," said Tilly, her shoulders still jiggling with amusement. "You were in such a daze standing there I just couldn't resist."

Zac couldn't help but laugh, too.

Tom reached out and turned the golden handle of the double doors, which creaked open. Beyond lay a gloomy, abandoned hall.

Tom stepped through the doorway, brushing aside a huge silken cobweb, and gestured for them to follow. Tilly and Zac stepped silently after him.

At once, Zac felt uneasy. Unlike the rest of HQ, it was cold and dark here — exactly the kind of place he imagined vampires and werewolves preferred — and he half expected another terrible monster to leap out of the shadows at any moment. He breathed deeply, forcing himself to follow the others through curtains of cobwebs. The floor was thick with dust, and scattered with footprints from the many times Tom and Tilly had sneaked through.

Some of the doors they passed lay open, and Zac glanced into the rooms. One looked like an abandoned classroom; another was a storeroom, piled high with ancient-looking chests. A third seemed to be an immense, disused library. He took a few steps into the room and looked up: The ceiling seemed miles away.

"Come on," whispered Tom, grabbing Zac by the arm.

Then he froze. A look of horror spread over his face.

"Tom, what are you looking like that for?" said Tilly. "That isn't funny. Stop it."

"Sshh!" hissed Tom.

"What is it?" asked Zac.

"Someone . . . someone's coming," spat Tom. "Quick! Behind here." He dragged them into the library, and they ducked down behind a desk piled high with books.

"Who is it, sneaking around at this time of night?" asked Tilly.

"How am I supposed to know?" snapped Tom. "Sshh!"

The door creaked open, and Zac heard stealthy footsteps moving through the darkness. Moments later, the door groaned again and a second person entered. Tom peeked over the edge of the desk. His eyes grew wide and he ducked back down instantly.

"It's Julius," he whispered, "and Gideon!"

"What in Nocturne are they doing?" said Tilly.

Zac looked out through the columns of books on the desk. Julius and tall, thin Gideon were standing in the center of the room. Gideon was furious.

"Well?" he snapped. "Would you care to explain exactly what you were doing back there, breaking into Tinn's quarters?"

"I . . . I was looking for something," said Julius. "Something I think might be rather important."

"Oh?" said Gideon. "Important enough to trawl through the Grandmaster's personal belongings?"

"Gideon, I think there may be a traitor among us. I was looking for something that might help me find out who."

Gideon was silent for a moment. "And did you find anything?" he finally asked.

"No. I hadn't been looking for very long when you burst in and dragged me down here."

"Oh, how convenient," said Gideon, raising an eyebrow.

"And what's that supposed to mean?" demanded Julius.

"Only that I find it very odd, Julius, that you would rather sneak around like a thief in the night than ask permission to enter Tinn's quarters. What would you have to hide if, as you claim, you have the interest of the Knights at heart?"

"Gideon, I swear!" pleaded Julius. "I was only trying to help. I didn't want to alarm anyone."

Gideon stared at him. He seemed to be making his mind up about something. "I feel that I would not be doing my duty if I did not ask you this question," he began. "Was it you that betrayed Tinn? Did you lead the Dream Stealers to him on the night of his capture? Please tell me the truth."

"That's ridiculous!" said Julius, scandalized. "I would never betray Grandmaster Tinn. He's like a father to me. He's the only one who can lead us against the Dream Stealers."

Gideon glared at him for a long moment. "Very well," he said at last. "I will give you the benefit of the doubt this time. But don't ever go sneaking into the Grandmaster's apartment again, or I will be forced to alert the others. And know that I am watching you, Julius."

Without another word, a pale and shaking Julius hurried away. Gideon watched him leave, then fished a handkerchief from his pocket and mopped his brow. After a few moments, he strode to the door and headed back up the corridor.

14

"You don't really think Julius could have betrayed Tinn, do you?" said a shocked Tilly as they climbed out from behind the desk.

"Who knows?" Tom replied. "But why would he be creeping around Tinn's rooms? That's pretty suspicious, if you ask me."

"Maybe he was telling the truth," said Tilly. "Maybe he was looking for evidence that one of us is a spy."

"Or maybe he was trying to destroy evidence that *he's* the spy," said Tom thoughtfully.

"Do you think we should say anything?" asked Zac. "You know, to Granny or the others?"

"I don't think that's a good idea," said Tilly. "The last thing the Knights need is to be suspicious of one another. I think Gideon handled it the right way. He'll keep this quiet, but he'll watch Julius like a hawk. If anything else happens, then he'll tell the others."

Zac nodded. "Julius just doesn't seem the kind of person who'd do something like that, though," he said.

"Let's just hope Gideon is wrong about him," said Tilly. "And in the meantime, I think we should keep an eye on him, too."

"Good idea," said Tom. "But there's nothing more we can do tonight, is there? So let's show Zac what we came to show him." He crept back over to the door, checked that the coast was clear, then led the others farther along the abandoned corridor. At the very last door, he stopped. It was covered in rusty chains and locks.

"What's in *there*?" said Zac.

"You'll see," said Tom with a smile. "Took us ages to get in. There don't seem to be any keys, so we had to practice unlocking things with magic for weeks. Tilly finally cracked it a few months ago."

"Is it hard using magic?" said Zac. He'd been wondering for a while. "How does it work?"

"Well, you have to concentrate hard on what you want to happen," said Tilly. "You have to see it clearly in your head. And then you feel this kind of warmth in your fingers, and, well, you just sort of know when the spell is ready to come out."

"But it is tricky," said Tom, "especially when you're trying a spell for the first time. If you don't concentrate, then it won't work, or something weird'll happen. I kept making locks blow bubbles. Mum and Dad went mental."

"Watch," said Tilly, and she held out her hand to the door.

A little wisp of smoke formed in her palm, and she blew it toward the door, where it poured into the locks. There was a series of clicks and rattles, and a moment later Tom pushed the door open, dislodging a plume of dust.

"Bravo, sis," he coughed.

The door led to a neat bedroom. There was a carefully made bed, and beside it a small round table. On the table stood a photograph in a wooden frame. Two people smiled brightly out at them. The first was a young man with a neat red beard. His arm was around the shoulder of a beautiful young woman with straight black hair and ruby lips.

"That's Rumpous Tinn in his younger days," said Tom, pointing at the picture.

"Who's the lady with him?" asked Zac.

"That's his sister, Aris," answered Tilly. "She was a

clever magician. A good one, I think. This was her room. Tinn doesn't speak about her much. She died years ago, pretty mysteriously, according to Grandad."

"Come on!" said Tom. "We didn't bring him here to look at old photos!"

Apart from the bed and table all Zac could see was dust. "There isn't much else here, though, is there?" he said.

"Well, no," said Tom, smiling smugly. "Not if you don't count this . . ."

He reached up and yanked one of the unlit torches on the wall. For a second nothing happened. Then, with a loud grinding noise, a small section of the wall started to move outward, leaving a square hole in the brickwork.

"Follow me," said Tom, crawling into the hole.

A moment later Zac heard his voice from the other side.

"It's OK, Zac, honest."

Tilly smiled and nodded encouragingly.

He knelt down and wriggled through the hole. When he was on the other side, Tom helped him up.

"Thanks," he said, dusting himself off. "So what exactly — Whoa!"

He was standing in some kind of laboratory. The shelves were packed with glass jars, all filled with powders, liquids, and body parts, like pickled eyeballs and spare toes. Textbooks, newspapers, and glass tubes were scattered all over the room.

"What is this place for?"

"We're not sure," said Tom. "Top secret magic stuff, we think. It looks like one of the apothecary shops in town, only some of these things are just plain disgusting." He picked up a small jar filled with a yellow-green gloop. "See what I mean? This one looks like it's filled with boogers! And what about this?"

He held up another jar. Zac peered at the contents and was amazed to see that it was crammed with row upon row of tiny sharp teeth.

"What are those?"

Tom studied the label. "Rats' jaws," he said faintly.

"Put those down, Tom!" Tilly had joined them in the secret room, and stood behind Zac, scowling at her brother. "You agreed not to touch anything after last time."

"Why?" said Zac. "What happened last time?"

"Oh . . . nothing," said Tom dismissively.

"Nothing?" said Tilly. "You turned your hair bright orange! We were searching for the antidote for hours."

"Look," said Tom, unscrewing the lid, "I've got to have one of these for my collection. How dangerous can they be?"

The words had no sooner left his mouth than the

top popped off the jar, and a set of needle-sharp teeth jumped out and attached itself to the end of his nose. Tom squealed and dropped the jar, which smashed on the floor, scattering shards of glass and rats' jaws, several of which chased him as he ran around, yelling and waving his arms.

"Keep still," said Tilly. She found a pair of tiny tweezers on one of the tables, then headed for her brother, kicking a few sets of rats' jaws out of the way for good measure. In one swift movement, she grabbed the offending set of teeth and pulled. Tom howled as the jaws lost their grip and flew across the room, where they landed on a high shelf and began to chatter angrily on the spot.

Pale and shocked, Tom rubbed his freckled face. There were tiny bite marks on either side of his nose.

"Thanks, sis," he said gratefully.

"Just don't open anything else," snapped Tilly.

Zac laughed and began carefully examining the contents of some of the other jars.

SQUID'S UDDER read one label. EXCELLENT FOR CONSTIPATION.

FLIES' WINGS AND FROGSPAWN read another. FANTASTIC FOR BREATHING FIRE.

Two small jars at the end of the shelf were stacked one on top of the other. The first held bright red pills and the label stated clearly: SALAMANDER AND SNAIL — SUPER FOR SHRINKING — TAKE ONE PILL TO REACH DESIRED SIZE. The second contained bright blue liquid and read GULLS' BEAK AND GREMLIN GUNGE — GOOD FOR GROWTH — TWO DROPS SHOULD DO THE TRICK.

"I wonder if these actually work," said Zac. He turned back to look at the others, but a glint of silver on a nearby table caught his eye. A strange feeling began to build in his stomach. And then he saw it. There, among stacks of books and newspapers, was the sapphire-encrusted dagger from his dream — the very one he'd used to attack the monster.

"Er . . . guys?" he said, carefully picking up the dagger. "Look at this."

"That's pretty," said Tilly. "Look at the jewels on the handle."

"I've seen this before," said Zac. "This exact dagger."

"How can you have?" said Tilly, frowning. "You've never been in here."

"It was in a dream," said Zac. "The dream I had tonight."

"You had a dream?" gasped Tilly. "Here? But people in Nocturne can't dream —"

"I know," said Zac. "Tom's already told me."

"But you told me you couldn't remember what your dream was about," said Tom.

"I didn't want to talk about it. It wasn't a very nice one."

"I knew it!" said Tom, looking rather excited. "It *was* a bad dream! So what happened?"

"Well," said Zac, "I was in a dark room and there was this black mist everywhere. All of a sudden, this dagger was in my hand."

He held up the dagger. Tom's and Tilly's eyes followed it.

"That doesn't sound too bad," said Tom.

"He's not finished yet!" snapped Tilly. "Go on, Zac."

"Then there were these heavy footsteps, and some kind of monster flew out of the darkness. I fell back, and the monster came down on the dagger and exploded. The dagger saved my life."

"Wow," said Tom, awestruck.

"It's probably nothing," he said, placing the knife back on the table, trying not to panic. "Hey, what were you looking at before I interrupted?" he asked, changing the subject.

"Oh," said Tom, tearing his eyes from the dagger. "This old trunk, it's locked tight. The lid won't budge. I'm dying to know what's in it."

He shot a hopeful look at his sister.

"I've told you a hundred times, I won't open it!" said Tilly, shaking her head in annoyance. "Judging by some of the stuff lying around this place, there could be anything in there."

"But it's a special occasion! We've got a guest."

"No!"

Tom scowled. "Fine. I'll try it myself. Again."

Tom crouched down by the trunk and closed his eyes in concentration. A moment later, a purple spark shot from the end of his finger and the lock began to spit out multicolored bubbles.

Tom shrugged in disgust.

Zac couldn't help grinning. "Go on, Tilly," he said. "Put him out of his misery."

Tilly glared at him for a moment, and then glanced at the trunk.

"Fine," she said. "I'll try, but it's probably protected."

Tom beamed at her. She marched past him and leaned over the trunk. Though she looked annoyed, Zac got the feeling that she secretly enjoyed showing off her talents. Another wisp of smoke appeared in her hand, and a moment later the trunk clicked open.

"Well, that was easy enough," said Zac.

But nobody answered. Tom and Tilly were gazing at the trunk's contents in fascination.

Zac edged closer. Heaps of small, roughly shaped spheres of thick colored glass were glowing inside the trunk, throwing a spooky light on Tom's and Tilly's faces.

"Dream orbs!" whispered Tom. "Sometimes these get left behind in the Dream Plains when a Wakeling has a dream. Each orb has an echo of a dream inside. I've never seen one up close before — no one's supposed to take them. There must be hundreds of them in here. And look, I don't believe it!" He reached over and carefully picked up one as if it were a small bomb. It was about the size of an orange, and looked like a huge black marble. Its surface was streaked with glowing purple waves.

"What's that?" asked Zac.

"A black dream orb," said Tom. "This is what's left behind if a Dream Stealer has been there — inside is a twisted dream."

Tilly's brow furrowed. "How do you know that?"

"*Myth and Magic*," Tom said. "Don't you *ever* read?"

"So it's dangerous?" asked Zac, eyeing the orb suspiciously.

Tom, who seemed to realize at that moment exactly what he was holding, held it out away from himself.

"Perhaps you'd better just put it down," said Tilly.

"I — I think you might be right," Tom agreed.

Zac and Tilly kept a safe distance as he began to put the orb carefully back into the trunk, but a tiny movement drew Zac's eyes to Tom's feet.

His heart almost stopped.

One of the runaway rats' jaws was snapping angrily around Tom's ankles.

Zac watched in horror as the little set of teeth jumped up and sank itself into Tom's foot. Tom squealed and performed a frantic tap dance on the stone floor, his arms flailing uncontrollably.

"Don't drop it!" Zac yelled. "Tom! Keep still!"

As Tom lost his grip on the black dream orb, everything seemed to play in slow motion. The orb began arching through the air.

"No!" screamed Tilly, diving at full stretch to catch it. But as she hit the floor, the orb smashed just beyond her outstretched fingers, releasing a cloud of billowing black smoke.

15

"You idiot!" yelled Tilly.

Tom backed away, his hands raised.

"Stop it, you two!" said Zac. "What is that stuff?"

The black cloud was growing by the second.

"Oh, no," moaned Tom. He slapped his own forehead.

"How bad is this, exactly?" asked Zac.

"We're about to find out!" yelled Tilly, shielding her face.

Everything went black as the fog engulfed them.

The only sound Zac could hear was the panicked breathing of his friends. He couldn't see them; the fog was impenetrable and yet somehow familiar. That was when he realized: He'd been here before.

"This is my dream!"

"What?" came Tom's voice.

"This is the dream I was telling you about."

"Erm, Zac, if this is your dream, then doesn't that mean that somewhere in this fog there's —"

A long, low growl sounded from close by, and the fog began to part.

"What are we supposed to do?" asked Zac.

They didn't answer. Tom was staring straight ahead, his mouth wide open. Tilly was looking in the same direction, her face a mask of terror.

Zac turned just in time to see the outline of a huge creature stepping from the fog. As it came into view, he tried to scream, but the sound stuck in his throat.

The monster was covered in stinking, matted gray fur. Glaring yellow eyes twitched and rolled in their sockets. A grizzled muzzle sniffed the air feverishly, and great globules of steaming drool dripped from a snarling mouth filled with teeth as big as steak knives.

"It's a werewolf!" squeaked Tom.

At the sound of his voice, the creature rushed at him. It was lightning quick, but Tom was quicker. Just as the monster reached him, there was a loud *pop,* and Tom vanished. The werewolf howled in anger and confusion.

"Where's Tom?" shouted Zac.

"Look down!" cried Tilly.

A field mouse was scurrying around the feet of the werewolf.

"That's Tom?" Zac hissed.

"Yeah," said Tilly. "Come on, it's going to squash him!"

She was right. The werewolf had spotted the mouse and was stamping hard on the ground in an attempt to crush him.

"Tilly, wait! Come back!"

It was too late. Tilly had crept up behind the monster and kicked it on the leg. It spun, covering her in drool, and swung at her with a huge arm.

"No!"

Zac sprinted forward, expecting Tilly to cry out, but all he heard was a growl from the werewolf. To his amazement, Tilly was standing exactly where she'd been. And she'd turned to stone.

The monster sniffed the air, catching a new scent. Zac felt his stomach fall to somewhere around his knees. He backed away, thinking of his dream. It had been just like this . . . only . . . where was the dagger?

As its image burned in his mind, Zac felt the dagger in his hand. Hardly daring to hope, he looked down to discover that he was clutching the blade. He swallowed hard and glanced at the werewolf. He guessed what was coming next.

"Hey! Over here!" he said, hardly able to believe that

he was actually trying to attract the monster's attention. "Fresh meat!"

The creature charged toward him, and fear flooded his body. The werewolf was too big and strong. He'd never be able to stop it.

And then he saw Tilly. She threw herself in front of the monster and turned to stone again as she hit the floor. The werewolf tripped over her and soared through the air. Zac fell backward, holding out the dagger. A gaping mouth of huge teeth loomed toward him. He closed his eyes.

BANG!

Smoldering ash floated in the air, twinkling like stars. The darkness faded, and Zac was back in the secret laboratory. Tilly lay on the floor, flesh and blood once more. He ran over to help her up. There was a *pop*, and Tom returned to his human form.

"That was brilliant, Zac!" he said. "How did you get the dagger?"

"I don't know," said Zac. "It was like in the dream. It just sort of appeared in my hand."

"Maybe you're more magical than you think," said Tilly.

"What about you?" Zac said. "You saved the day, tripping that thing up the way you did. How did you turn to stone like that?"

"I don't know, either," said Tilly, her cheeks turning red. "It's just what I do."

"Can you turn into anything you want?"

"Only what I'm touching at the time," said Tilly, "and then not for very long—especially if it's something I've never done before."

"Amazing," said Zac.

"Ahem," coughed Tom.

"Oh, yeah. And you can turn into a mouse," said Zac.

"Yeah," shrugged Tom. "It's all I can manage so far. Not very spectacular, is it?"

"I think it's pretty impressive," said Zac. "How many people can turn into different things the way you two can?"

"It's rare," said Tilly. "That's why Grandad was so desperate for us to be Knights."

"Hey, Zac," said Tom. "Maybe you should hold on to that dagger for a while."

"I can't do that," said Zac. "It doesn't belong to me."

"Aris Tinn is hardly going to miss it, is she?" said Tom. "Besides, you can put it back later. You'd just be borrowing it. Something tells me you're supposed to take it for now."

Zac stared at the dagger in his hand. As much as he thought it sounded ridiculous, he knew Tom was right. He felt as if the dagger had been waiting for him.

"All right," he said. "But I'm not keeping it for long. Just a day or two, right?"

"You bet," said Tom.

Zac slipped the dagger into the pocket of his robe.

"Let's get out of here," he said. "This place gives me the creeps."

"Agreed," said Tilly.

Safely back in bed, Zac slid the dagger under his mattress and lay awake, his mind racing. It was strange to think that, until last night, he hadn't even known Nocturne existed. It seemed like days since he'd followed Granny into the blizzard. He thought about the journey and The Forty Winks. He thought about the Knights and about the adventure he'd just shared with Tom and Tilly. He thought about the strange dream and the dagger. Was Tilly right? Did he have magic powers, too?

Tom snorted, and Zac glanced over at him. His mouth was gaping, and bubbles were escaping as he breathed. Zac grinned. He'd never had real friends before, but he was pretty sure he'd made a couple tonight.

16

Zac and Tom were awake very early the next morning and wasted no time before discussing the previous evening's adventure. After they'd relived every second of the battle with the werewolf, and examined the dagger, they moved on to the subject of Julius and just why he might have broken into Tinn's quarters.

"I still don't buy what he told Gideon," said Tom shrewdly. "I mean, looking for evidence that someone *else* is the traitor? Come on! Why wouldn't he just ask the others for permission to search Tinn's quarters instead of breaking in? I still reckon he was trying to cover his own tracks."

"Well, whatever he's up to, at least we know Gideon's

keeping an eye on him," said Zac. "And I think Tilly was right: *We* should watch him as well."

Their discussion continued as they walked to the dining room, where Mrs. Huggins had laid out a delicious breakfast.

"Good morning, lads," chimed Cornelius.

"Morning," said Zac. He plopped down on one of the large chairs, and began piling his plate with bacon and eggs.

Granny and Tilly were already in their places.

"All set for today, Zac?" asked Mrs. Huggins.

Zac looked over the sausage on the end of his fork. "All set?"

"To go into town and get you some new clothes," chuckled Mrs. Huggins. "We can't have you walking around in that bathrobe, can we?"

In all the excitement of the previous night Zac had completely forgotten about the trip into Slumber City. "Are you sure you can't come with us, Granny?" he said.

"I'd love to, lad, but I'm afraid I have to stay and practice some combat magic. I'm a little rusty, and I want to be at the top of my game should anything else go wrong."

Zac didn't like the sound of that.

"When are you leaving?" he asked.

"Tonight. The sooner we find Tinn, the better."

Just then, Gideon and Julius entered the room. Julius

was pale and flustered. Gideon seemed much calmer than he'd been the previous night, but he was far from his usual self.

Zac, Tom, and Tilly shot each other knowing looks as the pair sat at the table. Gideon proceeded to pile a small mountain of food on his plate, and began to dig in. Julius only took one piece of dry toast and nibbled the edges halfheartedly, his eyes barely leaving Gideon for a moment.

"I say, Julius, are you all right? You look ghastly," said Cornelius.

Julius dropped the toast on his plate. "I do feel a little queasy," he replied. "It's probably the thought of going by airship." He let out a nervous little laugh.

"Airship?" said Zac.

"That's how we're traveling," said Granny. "Young Julius has found a pilot who's agreed to fly us tonight."

Julius stood up so quickly that he knocked over a glass of orange juice.

"As . . . as a matter of fact, I really should get going," he said. "I'm due to meet the pilot and make arrangements. If you'll excuse me . . ."

While Julius hurried from the room, Gideon stared after him, his face grim.

"Poor lad," said Cornelius. "His nerves are shredded after what happened to Tinn."

"So," said Zac, "what's the plan, anyway? How are you going to find Rumpous Tinn?"

"We'll start in the North," said Cornelius. "The Dream Stealers won't be far from the Dream Plains. Their henchmen, the vampires, have been busy up there just recently. It makes sense that they'd keep him where they feel most secure. The hard part is finding out exactly where Tinn is hidden. Gideon has been working up in Port Town for a few weeks, doing what he does best. He's fallen in with some unsavory characters and tried to mine a little information."

"Have you discovered anything, Gideon?" asked Tom, perched on the edge of his seat.

Gideon smiled. "Well, actually, I have," he said.

The scraping of knives and forks fell silent. Everyone stopped eating, eager to hear what Gideon had to say.

"I've heard whisperings of some pretty gruesome things happening east of Port Town. Disappearances, murders . . . that sort of thing. As a matter of fact, I'm meeting an old chap there this evening, a former sailboat captain. Been everywhere, seen everything, you know the sort."

Cornelius and Granny nodded.

"Anyway," continued Gideon, "from what I'm told, he took his boat up north toward the mountains late last year, and when he returned, only half of his crew were still with him. He sold the boat the next day and retired. Won't speak a word of what happened. But rumor has it that his boat fell prey to vampires."

"Poor spirits," said Granny grimly.

"Where there are vampires, Dream Stealers usually aren't far away," Gideon reminded them. "I'll try to get the old chap to spill the beans on what became of his men. Hopefully it'll lead us somewhere."

"And we'll catch the airship and meet you in Port Town early in the morning," said Cornelius.

"There's an inn at the harbor called The Grumpy Dragon," Gideon said. "I'll meet you there. Hopefully I'll have something to report — and even if I hit a dead end, your idea might lead us somewhere, Cornelius."

"*You've* had an idea, Grandad?" said Tom, looking shocked.

"Indeed I have," said Cornelius. "Years ago, during the last battle against the Dream Stealers, Rumpous Tinn and his sister, Aris, began work on a pair of magical instruments."

He paused for dramatic effect.

Zac leaned in. "What were they?" he asked, unable to contain his curiosity.

"Locator compasses," said Cornelius. "Very special instruments indeed. Designed to point you in the direction of anything you might wish to find, or any place you want to go — anything, anywhere. Such gadgets would've been invaluable. They would have enabled us to stay one step ahead of the Dream Stealers. It was the sort of genius idea we'd all come to expect from the Tinns! But they could never get the compasses working, and poor Aris died before they could be completed. In honor of his sister, Tinn continued to work tirelessly on the project. Then, a year or so ago, he had a breakthrough. He completed one compass and was close to finishing the second, but when the Dream Stealer attacks began again, he thought it wise to hide both instruments. I don't know where he hid the finished compass, but I do know where to find the second one, and I think we can use it to help find Tinn."

He looked at Mrs. Huggins. "Holly will pick it up today when she's in the city. She'll be perfectly safe. Outside the Order, nobody in Nocturne knows it exists."

Tom broke the silence first. "But the second compass isn't finished?"

"Well," said Cornelius, "it is incomplete, but not useless. I have spoken to Julius. As Tinn's apprentice, he is closer to the Grandmaster's work than anyone, and he is hopeful that this compass will at least send us from Port Town in the right direction."

At this point, Gideon pushed his chair back from the table and jumped to his feet.

"We can only hope so," he said. "Now, I should be setting off if I'm to keep my appointment with the former captain. Even in my magic boat, it'll take me until midnight to reach Port Town. Cornelius, Mrs. Wonder, I shall see you there tomorrow morning. I hope you have a safe flight."

Gideon picked up his top hat from the table and placed it on his head. With his hat on, he almost touched the ceiling. He shot them his dazzling smile, and headed for the door.

17

After breakfast, Zac, Tom, and Tilly waited for Mrs. Huggins.

"Did you see the state of Julius?" said Tom. "He was so nervous I thought he was going to faint."

"I know," Zac said. "*And* he hardly stopped staring at Gideon, as if he was really scared of him."

"He left in a hurry, didn't he?" said Tilly.

"So did Gideon," said Tom. "I'll bet he wanted to keep an eye on Julius before he set off for Port Town."

"And what about this compass your mum is picking up today?" Zac said.

"I know," said Tilly. "It sounds amazing."

At that moment, Mrs. Huggins and Granny appeared, deep in conversation.

"Ready?" said Mrs. Huggins.

"All set," said Zac.

Granny ruffled his hair. "Have a nice time, lad," she said. "I'll see you when you get back."

Mrs. Huggins led the children through the door to the room with the trampoline floor. Zac waved back at Granny as the door creaked shut. They walked past the ends of the large chutes they had slid down the night before. But there didn't seem to be any way back up.

"Is there a staircase or something?" Zac asked.

"Stairs?" Tom repeated, as if it were the most ridiculous thing he'd ever heard. "Of course not. We've got something much better. Come on! Look!"

With that, he bounced away toward the door on the opposite wall and opened it, revealing yet another narrow chamber. There were tracks on the floor that ran the length of the room and bent sharply upward, leading through a hole in the wall and out of sight. On the track was a rusty metal bathtub on wheels.

"Climb in," yelled Mrs. Huggins, clambering over the side of the cart. Tom was next and Tilly followed him enthusiastically.

"Come on, Zac, dear," said Mrs. Huggins. "It's perfectly safe."

"You'll love it," Tom said, beaming.

Zac gingerly climbed aboard. It wasn't very comfortable with the four of them crushed in there, but he didn't have much time to think about that. After checking that the children were safely seated, Mrs. Huggins tapped on the side of the bath three times.

For a long moment nothing happened.

Then there was a crunching noise.

Then a *clunk-a-chunk-clunk*.

"Hang on, dears," said Mrs. Huggins. "Arms inside!"

Zac clutched the edges as tightly as he could, and felt some of the rusty metal come away. This didn't make him feel any better.

There was a sound like a giant blowing his nose and the cart went screaming up the tracks and through the hole in the wall like a bullet from a gun.

If Zac could have breathed he would have screamed. Instead, he settled for trying to keep his face attached to the rest of his body as the dark tunnel streaked past in a blur. There was an occasional yellow flash when they whizzed past a torch. Up and down and round they went, the underground air rushing through their hair, until they whistled around a corner and came to a jolting halt at a wooden platform. Barnaby the bartender was waiting, his large round face beaming as he reached down and helped them from the bathtub.

"Hello, Holly, my dear," he said. "Bang on time as usual."

"Morning, Barnaby," said Mrs. Huggins.

"Hi, Barnaby!" chimed Tom and Tilly.

"Good gracious, all of you!" He exclaimed, mopping the sweat from his brow with a silk handkerchief. "What a pleasure! Now, follow me, if you will."

He led them to the other end of the platform, where they climbed up some wooden steps and through a small trapdoor that led to the back room of The Forty Winks.

When they were all safely through, Barnaby dragged a stone slab over the trapdoor, concealing the entrance perfectly. They all walked out into the deserted pub.

"This is where I leave you," said Barnaby, unlocking the heavy front door and pulling it open.

Zac felt a wave of freezing air on his face. There was the smell of crisp, wintry wood fire, and the sounds of a bustling city.

"My word," said Barnaby, rubbing his hands together. "Looks like we had quite a snowstorm overnight."

He was right.

As they stepped from the warm pub out to the cobbled street, their feet crunched into new-fallen snow. Zac gazed around as people bustled and jostled between the quaint little shops and the crooked gingerbread houses.

In Daydreamer's Alley, Zac had to leap out of the way of a horse-drawn cart piled high with candy canes. A crowd of young children was giving chase. A woman brushed past him, dressed in thick fur and dragging a shining toaster on a red leash. It yapped and barked like a puppy as they passed. Granny was right: Some people really *did* have strange imaginations. He stared after the toaster until it was out of sight.

"Where're we going, Mum?" asked Tom.

"First stop is Fontooly's," answered Mrs. Huggins vaguely, scanning the window of a shop selling nothing but poisonous pets.

"Clothes shopping?" wailed Tom. "I hate clothes shopping!"

"You're the one who wanted to come along, Thomas," murmured Mrs. Huggins. "We have to get some clothes for Zac. Oh, that reminds me — here you go, dear."

She handed Zac a small cloth bag.

He peeked inside, finding — much to his revulsion — that it contained a pile of teeth. For a moment he felt a little weak, but then he remembered that teeth were money. Closing the bag carefully, he managed a half smile.

"Thanks," he said, although he wasn't quite sure if he meant it.

They walked on through a maze of twisting, snow-covered streets. There were stalls everywhere. One sold chocolate-flavored brussels sprouts. *What a good idea,* thought Zac, before his attention was grabbed by a grand building with a dazzling door sign that sparkled and fizzed: PONTIUS PULLERWICK'S PYROTECHNIC SUPERSTORE. The pavement outside was crowded with both children and adults watching miniature fireworks spit, whizz, and crack *inside* the shop window.

As Mrs. Huggins and Tilly chatted about clothes, Zac and Tom dropped behind.

"Tom," Zac said, "I've been wondering about something. How many Knights are there?"

Tom kicked at the pavement. "Not many now," he said. "Just us."

"How come?"

"It used to be different," said Tom. "Years ago, there were more. But when the last war with the Dream Stealers ended, Grandad says that people in Nocturne thought the threat was over." He rubbed his brow. "Stupid," he spat. "Nobody was interested in practicing good magic or becoming a Knight anymore. Nowadays most people only use spells to help with silly things like washing the dishes! They just let the Order fade away and didn't bother to think about what would happen if the Dream Stealers came back."

"So nobody here knows the Knights still exist?"

"A few people do," said Tom. "But most of them think we're a joke."

"And the Dream Stealers?" asked Zac. "Do people think that they're a joke?"

"Nobody wants to believe the Dream Stealers are back," said Tom. "But they're getting stronger. People can't pretend for much longer."

"Aren't you scared?"

Tom bowed his head. "A little," he said, then he raised his head and smiled hopefully. "But your granny's come back. That's the best thing that could have happened. She's given Grandad a boost because he knows Rumpous Tinn called her back for a purpose."

"That's what I'm worried about most," said Zac. "Now that the Dream Stealers have Tinn, what happens if they come looking for her?"

"Then we'll protect her," said Tom forcefully. "And anyway, from what Grandad has told me, your granny is one of the best magicians there is. She can look after herself."

"I suppose," said Zac.

"Almost there!" chirped Mrs. Huggins.

They were crossing a tall stone bridge. Below them, an enormous moat reflected the moody sky above. Looking up, Zac got his first proper view of Slumber Mountain, and saw that a tunnel had been blasted through its heart. *What on earth is that for?* he thought.

In answer a great rumble suddenly drowned out the hum of the street. Zac ducked, afraid the whole mountain was about to collapse.

"It's all right," said Tom with a chuckle. "It's just the Express."

He motioned upward, and Zac's eyes followed. A large, black steam train was swooping through the extraordinary tunnel, spewing out great clouds of purple steam. Behind it, a long row of carriages snaked through the air.

"Of course," said Zac. "A flying train. What else?"

A few minutes later, Zac was standing in front of a tall mirror in a very splendid shop. It was built on four golden levels around a waterfall and staffed by elves, who turned out to be the most dedicated and helpful shop assistants imaginable. The miniature man serving Zac even brought them all steaming mugs of hot chocolate with tiny marshmallows floating on top.

"What kind of style would sir like to try?" he asked, taking in Zac's reflection and raising his eyebrows at the robe-and-slippers ensemble.

"Er, I'm not sure," said Zac. He looked at Tom and Tilly in the mirror. "What do you think?"

Tom shrugged.

"Why don't you try a few different things, dear," offered Mrs. Huggins.

"A good idea, madam," said the elf excitedly.

"Fine," said Zac.

The elf gazed expectantly at him.

"Shall I choose some clothes?" Zac asked, embarrassed.

The elf looked at him as though he'd just spoken complete gibberish.

"That's not how they do things here, Zac," said Tilly. "Just look in the mirror."

Zac turned back to his reflection. The shop assistant grinned toothily.

"How about this, sir?" he said, snapping his fingers.

The tall mirror began to shift and warp as if someone were pouring water down its surface. When the glass cleared again, Zac squeaked in horror at what he saw. Although in reality he was still wearing his robe, the mirror showed something very different: He appeared to be dressed in a baggy pink fur suit with an enormous gold belt. A mass of ruffles exploded from a bright green shirt under his chin. It was a hideous combination — even worse than some of the most garish outfits Zac had seen around Slumber City.

Tom fell off his chair with laughter, clutching his stomach. He was laughing so hard he couldn't breathe, and he kept making snorting sounds that attracted the glances of passing customers.

Tilly turned away and covered her face, her shoulders quivering.

"Erm . . . I think I'll try something else?" said Zac, his cheeks now almost as bright as his suit.

"Of course, sir," said the elf, and he snapped his fingers again. Once more the surface of the mirror rippled, revealing another outfit. This one involved a lot of sparkly blue sequins, and a top hat that turned into an umbrella when it rained.

"This is better than when Grandad got his leg stuck down the toilet!" said Tom, still fighting for breath.

"Thomas!" said Mrs. Huggins. "Be quiet. Perhaps something a little less complicated, Zac, dear?"

Zac nodded gratefully, and pointed to a passing customer who was more plainly dressed.

"There!" he said. "Something like that."

The elf took one look at the man and turned back to Zac, deflated.

"Very well," he said with a sigh, snapping his fingers halfheartedly.

"I think this is better," said Zac, looking at himself wearing a pair of finely checked pants and a matching vest under a smart blue traveling cloak.

"Oh, very handsome," said Mrs. Huggins.

"I'll take them."

"Excellent!" said the assistant. He fetched a set of step-ladders and began feverishly taking Zac's measurements.

"Well," said Mrs. Huggins, "if you lot don't mind, I'll pop out for a few minutes." She tapped the side of her nose. "I'm just going to pick up the You Know What . . ."

With all the distractions Zac had almost forgotten Mrs. Huggins was collecting Tinn's unfinished magical compass.

She turned and smiled at the little shop assistant. "Kind sir, would you mind keeping an eye on these three while I'm gone?"

The elf saluted proudly. "Not at all, madam," he said. "Anything for a customer of Fontooly's."

"Thank you," she said, kissing her children on the forehead. "I won't be long." She gave Zac's arm a little squeeze, and disappeared into the crowd.

"Where's she got to?" Tom fidgeted.

"Keep still. She won't be much longer," replied Tilly shortly. "You saw how busy it was out there . . ."

Zac stepped out from behind a heavy velvet curtain

wearing his new clothes. He stood in front of them, shuffling uncomfortably. Tom let out a low wolf whistle. Zac hung his head.

"Sir looks magnificent," said the elf, scurrying around making sure the clothes fit perfectly.

The cashier was back on the ground floor. After paying for his new outfit with some of the disgusting teeth in his money pouch, Zac heard Tom and Tilly arguing again.

"Well," huffed Tom, "I say we go and find her! She's been gone for almost an hour!"

"We're staying right here like she said, Thomas!" hissed Tilly, trying to keep her voice down. "We don't even know where she went. *And* you know how busy it is outside. I'm the oldest and I say we stay here."

"You're only the oldest by a couple of minutes!"

The elf looked agitated. "I'm sure she'll be back soon," he kept repeating under his breath.

"What do you think, Zac?" asked Tom, desperately. "We should go, shouldn't we?"

But before he could answer, Julius appeared on the crowded shop floor. He was obviously upset, and when he finally spotted Zac and the others, he hurried toward them.

"Children!" he panted. "Thank the stars you're safe!"

There were dark rings around his magnified eyes.

Worry was etched into his face. Something was very wrong.

"What's happened?" Zac asked.

Julius turned to Tom and Tilly. "It's your mother" he managed to say.

Tom stepped back. "Mum?" he said loudly. "What's happened to Mum?"

Tilly said nothing. The color had drained from her face.

"She's . . . she's been attacked," stuttered Julius. "She's alive, but she's in a bad way."

"Where is she?" demanded Tom.

"In Sweet Dreams Hospital. Your father is already there."

Tom began to run through the shop, banging into people as he went. Zac, Tilly, and Julius chased after him.

"Oh, dear!" squeaked the elf, as he watched them rush out into the crowded city square. "Please do come again!"

18

Noelle sat up stiffly and shook the fuzziness from her brain. There was something weighing down on her. Then she looked and realized her legs were completely buried under a ton of rubbish. She wrinkled her nose in disgust and peeled a rotting fish head from her arm.

Rumpous Tinn was nowhere to be seen.

"Mr. Tinn? Hello?"

A mound of garbage shook beside her and Rumpous Tinn emerged, blinking sleepily. He looked at Noelle and his eyes shone.

"Noelle!" he said. "You're awake."

"Awake, yeah, and wondering why I'm buried in a pile of rancid leftovers," she said.

Tinn seemed to find this amusing. "I found this refuse pit just off the staircase. Those garbage chutes lead to the kitchen." He pointed to three large holes in the wall. "Putting aside the possibility that the smell might kill us, I thought this would be as safe a place as any to get some rest. These days, my magic is not as strong as it used to be. I needed to recharge my batteries after fighting those guards, and you were out cold. How are you feeling?"

"I'm fine," she said, ignoring the pain in her leg as she stood.

Images of the fight played in her mind. She'd taken on a mountain troll! What had she been thinking?

"Mr. Tinn," she said, "can I ask you something? Something about how you treated those Dream Stealers back there?"

"Of course," Tinn said with a smile.

"Well," began Noelle, "why did you leave 'em alive? They ain't nothin' but monsters. They tortured you, and they'd have done you in without a second thought. Why didn't you just use your magic to finish 'em off?"

"A good question," replied Tinn. "I uphold the rules of the Knights of Nod. As such, I have sworn to use magic only for good. I will certainly defend myself — but no *good* can ever come of taking a life, especially if there is another option. Those guards were already beaten. I ask you, Noelle, would we have been any nearer escape if I'd killed them?"

"No," said Noelle. "I suppose we wouldn't."

"Then there is your answer."

The old man struggled to his feet. It was unbelievable, Noelle thought, that he'd managed to defeat not one, but five Dream Stealers, and a mountain troll.

Maybe he *was* special. Maybe the Knights of Nod *did* exist. She shook her head. No. It'd take more than a couple of clever spells to change her mind. Let the old man get her out of this place; *then* she'd believe.

"We should get moving," said Tinn. "I think it is safe to assume that the Dream Stealers built this hideout relatively close to the Dream Plains so they'd have somewhere to stop for food and rest after a busy night's work. If that is the case, then we can expect more company soon."

"Mr. Tinn?"

"Yes?"

"You really think we'll get out, don't you?"

"I do," he said, and then he did something extraordinary. He reached into his bushy beard, rummaged around for a moment, and pulled out a small copper device that looked like a pocket watch. He flicked open the lid and whispered something. A moment later Tinn smiled at the gadget as though it were an old friend.

"What's that?" said Noelle.

"This is what's going to help us escape."

"Is it gonna fly us out over the Dream Stealer lake?" she said.

Tinn chuckled. "No, my dear girl. It is going to lead us to another way out."

"But there ain't another way. I told you."

"You are quite sure?"

She nodded.

"What about the goblins?" he said.

"What about 'em?"

"Well, you told me they sneak in and steal from the Dream Stealers."

"So?"

Tinn chuckled again. Noelle scowled. He was beginning to annoy her.

"So," he said patiently, "if they have a way in, they also have a way *out*."

Noelle's heart began to race. He was right!

"But even if that's true," she said. "How are we gonna find it?"

Tinn held up the copper gadget. "This is a locator compass," he said. "It is one of only two ever made. And it's something I'm rather proud of."

"What does it do?"

"It helps you find things," said Tinn. "It leads you to anything you wish to locate, anywhere."

Noelle's eyes fixed on the shining object in the old man's hand. She felt a rush of excitement. "Anything? How?"

"Well, you, or rather I — it will only work for me as I made it — simply ask it," said Tinn. "And the dial will point me in the right direction. Look, I'll show you." He reached back into his beard and pulled out a tiny gold button. "Throw this over your head."

"What?"

"Throw it away."

Noelle took the button and tossed it into the surrounding garbage.

Tinn held out the locator compass so she could see the dial.

"Lead us to the golden button," he said.

Immediately, the dial began to spin. After a few moments, it came to rest. Tinn climbed through the garbage, and Noelle followed. After they'd taken six or seven steps, the dial began to glow.

"Ah," said Tinn, looking around the garbage at his feet. "It should be here somewhere . . . yes, here we go."

He leaned over and plucked something from the debris, then held out his open hand. The button was nestled in his palm.

"Wow," said Noelle, "it really works!"

"It does. Now, enough of this, we'd better get a move on." Tinn cleared his throat, and spoke directly to the compass. "Show us the way to the goblins' secret exit."

The dial whirred into life again. This time, when it came to rest, it was pointing to the garbage chutes.

Noelle stared at the holes in the wall. Green slime was dripping from them.

"It must be broken," she said.

"It is operational, I assure you," said Tinn.

"So we've got to go up there?" she said, wrinkling her nose.

"It makes sense," said Tinn. "You may be invisible, but I can't just walk up the stairs."

He offered her his hand.

But in the blink of an eye, Noelle had disappeared.

The old man chuckled and climbed up into one of the chutes. It smelt of rotten cheese. "Are you still with me, Noelle?"

"You're enjoying this, ain't you?" she replied from out of thin air.

"Oh, it isn't so bad," he said.

"Yeah. Just what I was thinking," said Noelle with a sniff, and they began to climb.

19

Zac had seen many weird and wonderful things since his arrival in Nocturne, but as he stood on the edge of the moat around Slumber Mountain, it occurred to him that Sweet Dreams hospital might just be the strangest yet.

When they'd headed toward the bridge, he'd assumed the hospital was on the other side of the water. It never crossed his mind that it might actually be *on* the water. As it turned out, Sweet Dreams Hospital was a huge boat — an ocean liner to be precise — no doubt plucked from the dream of a Wakeling. It was painted deep purple and gold, and its enormous funnel was a giant cigar puffing out thick white smoke.

Julius led the children across the gangway onto the

ship. Gray water lapped against the hull far below. Once on board, they headed along a gleaming deck and through the entrance.

The interior of Sweet Dreams was as different from the hospitals of the Waking World as the exterior had been. Everything looked cheerful and colorful and warm. As they navigated through a maze of passageways — each step cushioned by a fluffy purple carpet — Zac was reminded of the luxurious hotels he'd seen in old movies. They passed waiting rooms filled with squishy sofas, bellhops carting luggage, and even a waiter carrying a mountainous ice-cream sundae.

The air smelt of cinnamon and fresh baking, and it made Zac think that if more hospitals in the Waking World were like this one, then perhaps people wouldn't be so afraid of them. Doctors and nurses hurried past in brightly colored uniforms, and as he passed some of the rooms, Zac couldn't help glancing inside. Patients here suffered from the strangest conditions. One man seemed to be growing fluorescent orange carrots from his nose, and there was a woman whose acid yellow hair was growing so rapidly it filled the entire room while nurses rushed around her with scissors, trying to keep it under control.

At last, they reached Mrs. Huggins's room. Tom

looked to his sister for support, then opened the door.

Inside, the Knights were crowded around a four-poster bed, each looking more tired and drawn than the last. Granny hugged Zac so tightly he thought he might end up in the next room as a patient.

"Mum!" whispered Tom and Tilly.

They rushed to the bed where Mrs. Huggins lay quite still. Her face was cut deeply down one side and her eye was swollen purple.

Mr. Huggins stood up quickly and embraced his children. "You can't wake her, kids," he said gently to Tom and Tilly. "She's been given a sleep serum. She won't come around for a few days."

"She's going to be OK, isn't she, Dad?" pleaded Tilly. Her eyes were streaming.

"Come on," said Granny to the others. "Let's go outside and leave them."

Zac followed his grandmother out into the corridor, where Julius joined them. Cornelius stayed in the room with his family.

"Granny," whispered Zac, "what happened?"

"She was attacked by Dream Stealers," said Granny quietly.

"Will she be all right?"

"We won't know that until she wakes up."

"But why Mrs. Huggins?"

"They were after the locator compass," said Granny. "And they took it."

"They tried to kill her," said Julius. He had turned a nasty shade of green and was trembling terribly. "But she managed to stagger out into a busy street, and the attackers fled."

"Wait a minute," said Zac. "How did the Dream Stealers find out about the compass? Cornelius told us that nobody other than the Knights knew anything about it." His eyes widened as he began to understand. There *was* a spy in the Order! What other explanation could there be?

"We're still trying to figure that out, Zac," said Julius.

Zac felt sick. Julius! Julius had left breakfast in a suspicious rush that morning. He'd known about the compass. Had he rushed away to tell the Dream Stealers? Had Gideon been right about him? If so, then Mrs. Huggins was lying in a hospital bed because of what he'd done.

"What's wrong, lad?" asked Granny.

"Nothing," said Zac, his voice shaking. "I can't believe what's happened, that's all. Where did Mrs. Huggins collect the compass from?"

"The Guardian's Guild," said Julius. "It's a maze of vaults. The doors and corridors keep changing places. If a person makes a deposit, only he or she will be able to find it again. Anyone else will only get lost. That's why Holly had to be the one to collect the compass. She was the one who left it there for Tinn in the first place."

"So the Dream Stealers knew where she was going and what she was doing?"

"That seems to be the long and short of it," said Granny.

Just then the door to Mrs. Huggins's room opened and the others came out to join them.

Tom's and Tilly's eyes were red and puffy, and Tom's freckled cheeks were still glistening with tears.

"Dad said the doctors think she'll get better," said Tilly quietly. "She might be a bit jumpy for a while, but hopefully it'll pass."

It had been decided that Mr. Huggins was to remain at Sweet Dreams with his wife, while the children went back to The Forty Winks and stayed with Barnaby. The attack on Mrs. Huggins hadn't changed the Knights' minds; it had just made them more determined to find Tinn. They'd be setting out at midnight.

As they left the hospital, Zac told Tom and Tilly what he'd learnt about the attack on their mother.

"Julius!" spat Tom. "The troll-dung-licking git!"

"He's going with them on the mission tonight!" said Tilly. "He's the one who's arranged the airship. What if it's a trap? What if he's leading them into danger?"

"We should tell them," said Tom. "We have to —"

"Nobody will believe us," said Zac. "Anyway, there's no actual proof that he's done anything wrong."

"Well, we have to do something!" said Tilly.

"Wait a minute," said Tom. "Zac, last night you had a dream that we'd meet a monster and kill it with a silver dagger, and it came true, right?"

"And?" said Tilly.

"Well, what if Zac could go to sleep and dream about what's going to happen next?" He looked at Zac, his face full of hope.

Zac's shoulders slumped. "I'm sorry, I don't think that's how it works," he said. "People can't choose what they dream about before they go to sleep. I didn't choose to have the dream with the werewolf, although I had been reading about them."

"But you can try, can't you?" said Tilly, clasping her hands together.

"Perhaps if I think about Dream Stealers just before I go to sleep . . . ," said Zac. "But don't expect it to work. Last time was just a coincidence."

"You're a star!" said Tilly, and she hugged him tightly. Zac felt as though his face was on fire.

"Look," he said, breaking free, "whether your crazy dream idea works or not, we still need another plan."

"I'm going with them," said Tom.

"What?"

"Tonight. When Grandad and the others leave, I'm going, too."

"Tom," said Tilly, "there's no way Grandad'll let you—"

"I don't care," said Tom matter-of-factly. "I'll stow away. You saw what the Dream Stealers did to Mum, Tilly. You saw her lying there, helpless. I'm going. I'll be on that airship."

"Grandad will go bonkers," Tilly said, putting her head in her hands for a minute.

Then she looked up at him determinedly. "Well, if you're going, so am I."

"OK," said Tom. "I just know we can help, sis. It doesn't matter how old we are, or how small."

"What did you say?" said Zac.

"What?" said Tom, looking puzzled.

"What did you just say?"

Tom gave his sister a funny look. "I—I said it doesn't matter how old or small we are."

"That's it!" said Zac excitedly.

"That's what?" said Tilly, raising an eyebrow.

"I've figured out a way for us to go along without anyone noticing."

"Whoa!" said Tom. "What do you mean by 'us'?"

"You're not going without me," answered Zac.

"Zac," said Tilly quietly, "it'll be dangerous."

Zac folded his arms. "We're in this together," he said.

Finally, Tom took a deep breath. "OK, you're in. Let's hear the plan."

Zac paused. "Remember those potions in Aris Tinn's laboratory? I think we could put them to use . . ."

That night, Zac lay awake, his head buzzing. He couldn't do it. He couldn't control what he dreamed about. It was impossible. And the more he thought about it, the less he felt he'd be able to sleep at all. He glanced over at Tom's bed. Tom was breathing deeply, but Zac knew he was only pretending, that he was lying awake, too, hoping Zac would be able to dream up something on Julius and the Dream Stealers. Zac began to panic at the thought of letting his friends down. He squeezed his eyes tightly, willing his brain to switch off.

Please, let me sleep, he thought. *Even just for a few minutes.*

It was no use.

He watched the flickering night-light and wished he knew how to do magic like everyone else here.

Tom snorted. He was still pretending to sleep. But it

reminded Zac that *he* was the only person in the entire world of Nocturne who could dream. That had to mean something. Perhaps he was special? He thought about his grandmother and how she had always believed in him. She had always been there. Whatever lay ahead, he promised himself, he would find a way to protect her. Comforted, he found his eyes were growing heavy and his chin was sinking onto his chest. He slept . . .

Zac found himself in a shabby corridor. A flash of light half blinded him, and something slammed into the wall above his head. A scream pierced the darkness. Crouching low, he ran the length of the passage, flinching as more flashes blazed through the gloom. He reached a doorway. The door had been ripped from its hinges. He rushed into the room and saw something or someone standing over a crumpled heap. The heap stirred, and Zac saw a familiar wrinkled hand reaching up for help.

Granny! She was in terrible danger.

20

"The kitchen's just ahead," whispered Tinn over his shoulder. "I can hear them working."

"Oh, good," replied Noelle, and she picked something green and slimy from her hair. They'd been covered in falling slop four times on their way up the chute.

A faint glow was visible above them, and they soon reached the top of the chute, which was sunk into the floor of the vast, steam-filled kitchen. In every corner, kitchen hands were working feverishly, preparing all sorts of delicious-looking food.

"The Dream Stealers certainly know how to eat well," said Tinn, eyeing a wild boar on a spit. There were rows and rows of black stoves, and on each one sat bubbling pots and pans.

"There must be a hundred pots," said Tinn. "How many Dream Stealers are in this place?"

"Hard to say," replied Noelle in a whisper. "It changes all the time. Most come and go. You've got a bit of spinach in your beard, by the way."

Tinn felt around his chin and removed a soggy leaf.

"How do we get through the kitchens without 'em seein' you?" asked Noelle. "I mean, I can do it easy. I've done it a thousand times. But what about you?"

Tinn quickly peeked out of the chute. "What we need," he said, stroking his beard, "is a diversion."

"What kind?" asked Noelle. "Look out!"

She tugged him back below floor level in the nick of time.

A pair of worn black boots stomped over to the chute.

Noelle held her breath, and just as well, because the Dream Stealer tipped the contents of his bucket into the chute, dunking Tinn and Noelle in the stickiest, smelliest swill yet.

Tinn spat out a moldy lump of bread. "This is growing tiresome," he said. "Time to go, I think."

Once again he reached into his beard, and this time produced a tiny paper package. He unwrapped it. In the crease were dozens of teeny black balls. Noelle thought they looked like miniature peppercorns.

"What are those?"

"These are our diversionary tactic," said Tinn with a smile. "Have you ever seen fireworks?"

"No."

"Ah. Well, these were purchased from Pontius Pullerwick, the finest firework-maker in all of Slumber City. Watch this."

He held the fold of paper up to his mouth and looked Noelle dead in the eye.

"When I say go, we go."

He took a deep breath and gently blew. The tiny balls scattered through the kitchen, whining like a cloud of mosquitoes. In just a few moments they had dropped into every pot in the room, and the Dream Stealer chefs were unwittingly stirring them in.

"Get ready," whispered Tinn.

Noelle made herself invisible, preparing to run.

Then it happened.

Fizzing light exploded from every pot in the kitchen in a shower of steaming grub.

It was chaos. The kitchen hands were screaming. Some were covered in food, while others ran around with pails of water in an attempt to extinguish the light show.

"Go!" said Tinn.

He and Noelle scampered from the chute across the kitchen, keeping low and darting from stove to stove until they reached a heavy door on the opposite side of the room. Tinn pointed at the door and it swung open.

Then he froze.

In the doorway stood a guard who'd rushed to see what all the fuss was about. Behind his skull mask, the Dream Stealer's eyes gleamed. But before he could raise the alarm, a huge metal frying pan flew off the wall of the kitchen and landed on his head with a clang. The Dream Stealer crumpled. Tinn leapt over his body and out into the corridor, slamming the door on the bedlam behind.

The air fluttered. Noelle became visible and strolled up to Tinn, swinging the frying pan like a tennis racket.

"No need to thank me," she said smugly.

"Good work," he said, grinning.

She skipped with pride behind the old man as he led her out into a hexagonal chamber. Six silver doors stood glinting before them.

"Which one?" said Noelle.

"Let's ask the compass." He held out the shining device. "Which door will lead us to the goblin passage?" he asked.

The dial whizzed around. When it stopped, it pointed at a door to the left.

"We have our answer," said Tinn.

"Then let's go," she said, wondering where it would lead them next.

Tinn paused. "Noelle," he said, "I must warn you; the next stage won't be an easy one. I cannot guess what we will encounter along the way."

"Mr. Tinn," Noelle said, "I've lived in this stink hole for almost my entire life. It's gonna take more than a few goblins to stop me. I'll walk to the center of the world if there's a way out on the other side."

21

"I did it! I had another dream," said Zac, jumping out of bed in his urgency to get dressed.

"I told you, didn't I?" said Tom, impressed both by Zac's talent and the genius of his own idea. "Well? What did you see?"

Zac felt his heart beat as he told Tom about the dream. He described the dingy corridor, the helpless heap on the floor. "It was just a snapshot," he gasped. "But the one thing I feel for certain is that Granny and maybe the others are in terrible danger." He glanced at the windup clock on Tom's desk. It was almost midnight. "Time to go," he said.

Tom, who'd been watching him carefully, folded his

arms. "Are you sure about this, Zac?" he said. "You don't have to come, you know. Tilly and I can go. This is our world, our fight."

"If Granny is in trouble, it's my fight, too," said Zac. "And she's told me what'll happen to the Waking World if the Dream Stealers win — all that pain and suffering because people can't sleep. I'm not going to stand back and let Julius lead her into a trap. You're fighting for your mum and your family. Well, Granny's all I've got."

"You don't have a mum?" said Tom.

Zac pulled the traveling cloak he'd bought at Fontooly's more closely around him.

"She died when I was born. I guess my dad didn't fancy looking after me on his own, because he dumped me with *his* mum — Granny Wonder — when I was just a baby. That was eleven years ago, and she's looked after me ever since. That's why I have to come with you. I owe it to Granny. I need to know she'll be all right."

There was another reason Zac was determined to stay with Tom and Tilly. He felt a connection to this strange, wonderful place, a bond he couldn't quite describe.

"You're right," Tom said, "you should come along. I was just trying to help."

"I know," said Zac. "Thanks. But you're forgetting something else — this plan was my idea. I'm not letting you and Tilly take all the credit!"

Tom grinned. "Hey, it hasn't worked yet," he said. "And don't forget to bring that . . ." He pointed to the blade on the bed. The sapphires seemed to glow.

"All right," said Zac, slipping the blade into his cloak, "but I hope I don't have to use it."

They crept out into the grand corridor, where they distantly heard Granny and the others preparing for their mission. When they reached the entrance to the abandoned passageway, Tom jammed a piece of parchment under one of the doors to keep it open a fraction.

. Tilly was already waiting by Aris Tinn's laboratory. Tom told her excitedly about Zac's latest dream and how he thought the Knights were definitely heading into danger. Tilly let out a horrified squeak and unlocked the door at once.

Minutes later, they were examining bottles, jars, and tubes on the shelves of the secret room.

"Look for a bottle of bright red pills and some blue stuff — and stay away from that thing this time," said Zac, glaring at the trunk of dream orbs.

"Good plan," said Tilly. "Hang on, I think I've found them already." She grabbed two small bottles from a shelf and read the little white labels: "SALAMANDER AND SNAIL — SUPER FOR SHRINKING and GULLS' BEAK AND GREMLIN GUNGE — GOOD FOR GROWTH."

"Those are the ones!" Zac said.

"What are you thinking? We can't swallow them. What if something goes wrong?" shrieked Tilly.

"Look," said Zac, "I'm not exactly crazy about the idea of swallowing this stuff, either. Tom can turn into a mouse, but it's the only way I can think of for us to tag along with Granny and the others without being seen."

Tilly thought for a moment, and then made a grab for the bottle of red pills. "All right," she said.

Zac snatched them away from her. "No way," he said. "This was my idea. I'll go first. If anything goes wrong, it's going to happen to me."

He slipped the bottle of electric blue liquid into his pocket, then unscrewed the cap from the second bottle and tipped one of the little red tablets into his hand. Tom and Tilly held their breath.

"Here goes," said Zac with a shrug. He popped the pill into his mouth and tossed the bottle to Tilly.

The taste was so sour it drew his jaws together and almost made his face turn inside out. After a moment a tingle began in his toes and spread upward until his whole body was prickling.

Then there was a loud *ZING*.

Tom and Tilly looked at each other in amazement.

Zac had disappeared.

"Where is he?" said Tom.

"Sshh," snapped Tilly, holding up a finger. "Listen."

They stood in silence.

"I'm here!" said a tiny voice.

Tilly peered down at the floor. "Sweet starlight!" she exclaimed. "I can see him. It worked, it really worked!"

Under the table in front of them, Zac was crouching behind one of the wooden legs. He stood only an inch or two tall, and was waving wildly.

"Well," Tilly said, "here goes," and she swallowed one of the pills. There was a second ZING and Zac found Tilly standing beside him, looking up at Tom. He seemed to be a hundred feet tall.

"Wow!" said Tilly. "This is unbelievable! Look how big everything is. I'll never make fun of Tom for being a squirt again."

"I'm just glad our clothes shrunk with us," said Zac, patting his cloak. "I was a bit worried about that."

"Hang on!" Tom yelled. "I'm coming." His voice was so loud and booming Zac and Tilly were almost deafened. In the blink of an eye, Tom turned himself into a mouse.

Tilly fished a timepiece from her coat pocket. "It's almost midnight," she said. "We have to go, or we'll miss our chance."

"Jump on my back," said Tom. "It'll be much quicker . . . Ouch! Careful, you two, you're pulling my fur."

There were whispered apologies, and Tom scampered into action. They shot out of the laboratory, through the bedroom, past the old library, through the gap in the door, and back into the main corridor.

"You think we're too late?" asked Tom nervously.

"No," said Tilly. "Listen!"

They heard the voices of Granny and the Knights on their way to the room with the trampoline floor.

"Quick!" yelled Zac. "Follow them through the door!"

Tom darted through behind them, dodging nimbly between their feet. As they walked, the Knights discussed their task.

"So," said Cornelius, "this pilot, what's his name again?"

"Rigby Sundown," said Julius. "He's meeting us upriver. Thought it'd be safer than one of the airship stations. You never know who's watching."

"He'll be there, will he? You're sure?"

"I only gave him half his fee," said Julius. "If he wants the other half he'll be there."

Back on the floor, Tom was finding it difficult to navigate the bouncing surface and avoid being crushed beneath the Knights' gigantic feet. After a few close calls, they made it into the small chamber where the bathtub stood waiting.

"Oh, no," whispered Zac. "How could I have forgotten we'd have to ride in that again?"

"How do we get in?" said Tom, his whiskers twitching.

"The sides are far too slippery to scramble up."

They watched as the three Knights clambered in.

"Look," said Tilly. "There's a gap underneath. We could squeeze in there."

She was correct, as usual. The bathtub sat inside a metal frame on wheels, and there was a space between the two. It was only a few inches at most, but it was roomy enough for a mouse.

Tom's stumpy mouse legs helped him scrabble up easily, then he turned and helped Zac to hoist Tilly on board. Just as Tilly landed, there were three thunderous thumps that seemed to shake the whole room.

"We're about to go!" squeaked Tom in a tiny, panicked voice. "Hurry up, Zac, c'mon!"

The cart was already beginning to move. Zac sprinted after it. As it picked up speed, his lungs burned and his muscles ached. He couldn't push his miniature legs any faster.

Held in Tom's teeth, Tilly leaned dangerously out of the bathtub toward him.

"Jump, Zac!" she yelled. "JUMP!"

Zac leapt toward the cart. Tilly's hand caught one wrist.

"Whose idea was this?" he said.

"Hold on!" shouted Tilly over the roar of the wheels on the track. "We're going to swing you up. On three . . ."

Zac felt himself being swung backward and forward, building momentum.

"One!"

She was quite strong for a girl.

"Two!"

"I've changed my mind!" he yelled.

"THREE!"

As Zac landed, the bathtub suddenly burst forward in a breathtaking lurch of speed. They'd made it: well, as far as the front door of The Forty Winks, anyway.

At the front door, they watched as Granny stopped next to a peg where several fur coats were hanging. She took one and slipped it on.

"It's still freezing out there," whispered Tom. "We'll never be able to walk through the snow quickly enough to keep up."

"We've got to get into one of those coats," said Tilly. "Inside a pocket or something."

"Leave it to me," said Tom, and he scrambled away.

The longest coat was trailing on the ground, and Tom bounded up to it and began to chew into the lining. In a matter of seconds there was a hole just big enough for him to squeeze through. He climbed in and poked his head back out at them, his whiskers twitching proudly.

"How does he manage to look smug, even as a mouse?"

puffed Tilly, leaping gaps in the floorboards as she and Zac ran toward her brother.

As soon as they were all safely inside the coat, they felt it being lifted from the peg and heard Cornelius grumbling about it being itchy.

"Guess this is Grandad's coat, then," said Tom, grinning.

They felt the swish of the coat as Cornelius put it on, and heard the front door being unlocked. Then the door of The Forty Winks slammed behind them and they were off, peering out at the falling snow, as the Knights of Nod trudged through the city streets.

22

It was after one a.m. when they reached the harbor, and the snow was falling harder than ever.

Julius led them to the water, where he'd arranged for a rowboat to be moored. They climbed aboard and Julius untied the boat, setting them adrift. Cornelius picked up the oars and propelled them out toward the huge city gates. A security troll passed them without incident, and soon they were out on the vast river, so calm and black it looked like a puddle of oil.

When they'd rowed upstream a little, Julius said, "He should be waiting just over there, beside the old candy-cane lighthouse. Ah, yes — I can see a campfire."

"That's a start," laughed Cornelius. "At least he turned up."

As the boat bobbed across the great river, Zac and the others nestled into the lining of Cornelius's coat and listened to the Knights talk about the pilot Julius had found to fly them to Port Town.

Rigby Sundown was known to be the finest sky captain anyone could ever hope to find. He'd escaped bandit skywaymen a hundred times, or so the stories went, although he'd been badly injured on more than one occasion. He'd flown farther over the Eternal Forest than anyone in history—at least, anyone who'd come back.

"Ever been on an airship?" Zac asked Tilly and Tom in a whisper.

"Never," they both replied.

"Always wanted to, though," said Tom.

"Imagine soaring above the clouds with the dragons and birds," Tilly said dreamily.

"What about those bandits, though?" said Zac.

"Skywaymen?" said Tom, a faint smile creeping over his face.

"Yeah. I take it we don't want to come across them?"

"I'll say," said Tilly. "They're supposed to be ruthless."

"They're pretty rare now," said Tom. "But I'd love to see them just once."

"You must have a screw loose," snapped Tilly. "They're all thieves and murderers."

"I know," said Tom happily. "I've read all about them in —"

"*Myth and Magic*?" guessed Zac.

"Yeah!"

Zac said nothing more, but *he* certainly didn't want to encounter any skywaymen. He took comfort from the fact that Rigby Sundown had escaped them so many times. And of course, Granny and the Knights would be there, too . . .

Cornelius brought the rowboat to a halt in the shallows, and the Knights ventured up the bank to a simple campsite that smelt of damp firewood. Zac peered out through the hole in the coat's lining. There was a tent shaped like a tepee, and, less encouragingly, some dirty dishes and scattered bottles of rum.

"Hello," Julius said. "Hello, Mr. Sundown?"

There was no answer.

A snarling blur among the snowflakes made them all jump. In a heartbeat, a huge wolf was on top of Julius, its teeth almost at his throat, its eyes glaring right into his. Julius let out a little moan.

A gruff voice thundered from the tent. "Maggie! Maggie, get down!"

The tent flap opened to reveal a man sitting in a makeshift chair with wooden wheels, his face thrown into shadow by the campfire. Dark brown eyes were just visible behind a curtain of straggly gray hair. He wheeled himself forward, and raised a hand encased in a fingerless glove to rub his stubbly chin. The flames lit his weather-beaten, scarred face for a moment, revealing the remnants of lost good looks, buried under many years of battle.

"Maggie," he ordered the wolf. "Release!"

The animal was at the man's side in an instant.

Rigby Sundown gazed at the Knights and smiled crookedly.

"You'll be my fare, then, eh?"

"Erm, yes, yes," said Cornelius, taking a step forward and extending his hand. The wolf growled again, and he hastily withdrew it.

"You got the rest of my fee?" the man demanded.

Granny signaled to Julius, who produced a leather pouch and handed it over to the pilot. He scanned its contents.

"Seems fine," he muttered, and tossed the bag to his wolf. She caught it in her jaws and took it into the tent.

"So," said the man, "you need me to take you to Port Town, eh?"

"That's right," answered Granny.

"Just the three of you?"

"Yes," said Granny. "I'm Eve Wonder." She motioned toward the others. "These are my friends, Cornelius

Huggins, and of course you've already met Julius."

The man nodded. "Rigby Sundown," he said gruffly.

"Mr. Sundown," said Cornelius, "we'd prefer to be off as soon as possible."

"The ship's ready to go," Sundown answered. He took a flask from a pouch on the side of his wheelchair and helped himself to a long draft. "What's your business, if you don't mind me askin'?"

"That is not your concern," said Cornelius.

"Hmm," grunted Sundown, "when I'm asked to undertake a voyage in the dead of night over dangerous skies, riskin' my own ship and my own neck in times like these . . . well, I'd say that makes it my concern."

Cornelius sighed. "We're looking for a friend," he said.

"He's been captured," said Granny. "By Dream Stealers."

Sundown's eyes narrowed. "Dream Stealers?" he breathed. "Makes sense. Bad things been happenin'."

"Maybe you've seen him, or heard something?" said Cornelius hopefully. "His name is Rumpous Tinn."

"Can't say as I have," said Sundown. He wheeled away. "*Nightstalker*'s just over here. I hid her in some trees."

"*Nightstalker*?"

"My ship," said Sundown. "Maggie! Let's go!"

The wolf reappeared, trotting beside the pilot as he led the Knights of Nod up to a wooded area.

"Wow!" said Tom, poking his head out next to Zac's. "This thing is amazing!"

Granny and the others were standing in a clearing. In the center of it sat a rusty camper van. Its cream paint was peeling, and various pieces of equipment were barely hanging on — including a pair of nailed-on rickety wings that seemed to be made of wood and canvas. On the side of the old van, the word NIGHTSTALKER had been painted in untidy gold letters.

"That's it?" Zac said, beginning to panic. "*That's* the airship?"

"Why?" said Tom. "What's the matter?"

"It's not even meant to fly! It's a camper van. Where I come from, they just stay on the ground."

"That's a bit boring, isn't it?" said Tom.

"I'm sure it'll be fine, Zac," said Tilly. "These sorts of things pop out of the Dream Plains all the time."

Zac thought of the old bus that had floated past them on the river the day before.

"I suppose so," he said faintly.

"Hey, look, we're going in!" said Tom.

Sundown had pulled a handle, and a door had fallen open, turning into a ramp. The pilot wheeled himself aboard and motioned for the others to follow.

The inside of the ship was cramped and cluttered, and contained an unmade bunk bed, various items of scattered clothing, more empty rum bottles, and three worn leather chairs jammed together behind the driver's seat. A panel on the floor had been cut out and replaced with thick glass.

Sundown took his place at the wheel, twiddling knobs and flicking switches in preparation for departure. There was a great rumbling as the engine started, and the entire airship trembled. Granny and the others buckled themselves in just as Rigby Sundown pulled on a red lever, and *Nightstalker* heaved itself into the air. Zac felt his stomach drop as they climbed farther and farther from the ground. He glanced at Tom and Tilly.

"There's no going back now," he said.

23

Shadow stood at the wide window of an impressive manor house near the summit of Slumber Mountain. She stared down at the twinkling city.

Something caught her eye. Just beyond the city walls, the winking light of an airship lifted off from the banks of the river like a firefly. She watched until it had disappeared into the clouds, then she turned back into the room.

Gliding gracefully past a roaring fire, she took a seat at a wooden table. A pale, terrified-looking man sat opposite. Shadow stared at him from behind the lifeless black lenses of her skull mask. Finally, she spoke.

"So, Mr. Grub," she said. He flinched at the sound of

her voice. Every syllable cut through the air like a rusty razor. "In the time it has taken me to travel home from the North, Rumpous Tinn has escaped from our custody. He has beaten several of our guards in combat, even in his weakened state, and—oh, yes—he also subdued a mountain troll. Have I heard you correctly?"

The man was now shaking. "Y-yes, my lady," he managed to stammer.

"Is there anything else?" she asked calmly.

"No, my lady."

Silence.

"It's only a matter of time before we catch him," added the man in desperation. "He's trapped somewhere. We'll find him. And you have my word that this will never happen again."

Shadow's hex flew out toward him so quickly it was a blur. Grub was paralyzed. Only his eyes could still move, and they blinked desperately.

Shadow stood up and strolled around the table until she was right behind him. She placed a gloved hand on his shoulder.

"Mr. Grub, Tinn is gone. He will not be found unless he wishes it so. You were, however, correct about one thing: It will never happen again."

Something flashed in the firelight and Grub slumped to the floor in a lifeless heap. Shadow leaned over the body and wiped her dagger on his clothes. There was a knock at the door. She straightened up and replaced the knife in her cloak.

"Enter."

Shadow's housekeeper, a tall blond woman with ashen skin, entered the room. She took a few steps toward Shadow, but faltered when she spotted the body on the floor.

"Is everything all right, my lady?" she asked.

"Fine," said Shadow dismissively.

The blond woman tore her eyes away from the gruesome sight.

"The vampire has arrived, my lady," she said. "Shall I show him in?"

"Let him wait," said Shadow. "Do you have it?"

"Yes, my lady. We retrieved it yesterday, as you asked." The woman reached into her pocket and drew out a little pouch. Shadow took it from her and carefully pulled open the strings, emptying its contents into her hand. A small copper object sat in her palm. She held it up to the fire to examine it.

"My lady . . . ," said the housekeeper, hesitantly.

"Yes?" said Shadow.

"Why do you wish to possess an instrument that doesn't work?"

"Does not work *yet*," corrected Shadow. "This

trinket—this so-called compass—could very well be the key to our ultimate victory. It will help us to seek out and destroy the Trinity—the only three people who stand between the Dream Stealers and supreme power in Nocturne. We must find them!"

She stowed the locator compass in her cloak and took a seat at the table once more.

"I am ready. Send him in," she said, waving her hand.

"Yes, my lady."

The housekeeper disappeared through the door. A moment later, a man strolled into the room. He was tall and broad, with high cheekbones and cropped silver hair. His bloodred cloak trailed on the ground as he walked.

"Please sit," said Shadow.

The man caught sight of Grub's body on the floor. Seeing the pool of blood, he licked his lips.

"Sit *down*, Raven," said Shadow.

The man obeyed.

"My spy was correct," Shadow went on. "Those fools, the Knights of Nod, are on their way to Port Town. They left only minutes ago. They will arrive by morning."

Raven leaned forward. "My lady," he said, "the vampires are at your service, as always."

"Good," she said, "because I have a job for you. The Knights are traveling with an old woman called Evegenia Wonder. It seems that she has been stashed away in the

Waking World for the last fifty years. *I wonder why?* One can only assume now Tinn has brought her back that she's an important part of their plans — and a danger to ours. I have dispatched a crew to intercept the Knights in Port Town. Their orders are to capture this woman. They will bring her to you. You will guard her until I arrive . . . It is *very* important that I get to question her, Raven."

"Very well, my lady," Raven said. He paused for a moment. "May I ask which crew you have sent?"

"The werewolves," said Shadow.

"Werewolves! They will rip her apart before they deliver her! I think you would have been wiser, my lady, to send vampires. It can still be arranged."

"The werewolves will keep *her* alive," said Shadow. "They know what will become of them if they do not."

"But why werewolves?" said Raven, obviously disgusted.

"Because werewolves play with their food," said Shadow. "The Knights will beg for death before the end."

She stood and motioned to Grub's lifeless body.

"Do with him as you wish," she said. "Just clean the blood from the walls when you are finished."

"Thank you, my lady," said Raven, his lip curling to reveal an enormous pair of fangs. "This Evegenia Wonder will be held, as you command. I will not fail you."

Shadow's black eyes glittered. "You had better not."

24

Tinn peered at the locator compass. It had led them deeper and deeper underground. The previous hall-ways, resplendent in silver and crystal, had given way to suffocating earthen passageways. Noelle wasn't even sure they were in the Dream Stealer lair anymore.

For hours, they had been following the twisting path of an underground stream, and they had lost all sense of how far or how deep into the earth they'd traveled.

After walking in silence for a time, Noelle couldn't keep quiet any longer. Something had been nagging at her, a question.

"Mr. Tinn?" she said, aiming a kick at a small stone. "Can I ask you something?"

Tinn walked onward, glancing at her from the corner of his eye. "You may."

"In the torture room," she said, "when Shadow was . . . you know . . . you kept shouting something. A name."

"Did I now?" Tinn felt a throb in his temple.

"Yeah. Who's Aris?"

Tinn slowed slightly. He didn't look at her.

"It's OK," she said, sensing that she'd asked something very personal. "I mean, if you don't wanna tell me, that's fine. It ain't my business anyway . . ."

"Aris was my sister," said Tinn softly.

"You have a sister?"

"*Had* a sister," replied Tinn. "A twin sister, actually, but we weren't very alike."

"How d'you mean?"

"In terms of magical ability, we were equals," said Tinn. "I may have been a shade more talented, but Aris was much more ambitious and hotheaded." He shook his head. "She was so determined to rid the world of Dream Stealers that it began to consume her — and she became fond of breaking the rules to aid her cause."

"What happened to her?"

"She was killed," said Tinn, his pace quickening again. "Many years ago."

"Who killed her?"

"Well, when we found her, there were bites on her neck," said Tinn. "We also found the body of a vampire close by."

"A vampire did it?"

"It appeared that way, yes," said Tinn.

"Just like my village," said Noelle. "Were the vampires workin' for the Dream Stealers back then, too?"

"All dark creatures gravitate toward the Dream Stealers," said Tinn. "They are natural allies. But this particular vampire — the one we found close to Aris's body — was a friend."

Noelle stopped dead, her mouth open. "*You* were friends with a vampire?" she said. "How come?"

"It was complicated," said Tinn.

"And he killed her?"

Tinn let out a great sigh. "We will probably never know what really happened."

They walked on in silence for a minute or two, before Noelle spoke again.

"Is there gonna be another war, Mr. Tinn?"

"I am afraid it has already started," said Tinn. "The Dream Stealers are more determined than ever to gain control of Nocturne and the dreams of the Waking World. We cannot stand by and let that happen."

For a moment the only sound was that of their footsteps on the hard, wet stone.

"And you'll win, right? You and the other Knights?"

Tinn stopped in his tracks and looked at her, his eyebrows raised. "Ah," he said. "So you *do* believe in the Knights now?"

She shuffled her feet. "Well—yeah. I mean, I ain't sure yet," she said. "But I've seen you do things I've never seen anyone do before. *And* you've got that compass."

Tinn smiled, his worn face creasing. "I am glad you are coming around," he said, and he chuckled to himself as they continued to follow the path of the winding stream.

25

Nightstalker had hit a snowstorm.

Sundown fought again and again to bring his shuddering ship under control. With every roll and dip, Granny and the other Knights were thrown together. And Cornelius, his head resting on Granny's shoulder, had turned a horrible shade of green.

Granny gently nudged him onto Julius. She unbuckled her seat belt and climbed forward into the copilot seat beside Sundown.

He cast a sideways glance at her.

"How long have you been flying, Mr. Sundown?" she asked, peering through the windscreen at the wall of driving snow.

He didn't turn to face her. "Long as I can remember," he answered. "Grew up with my pa on merchant ships. When skywaymen killed him, I had nowhere else to go. The sky became my family. I got my own ship, an' the freedom that comes with it." He patted the steering wheel.

"But how were you injured?" inquired Granny.

"It was during the last war," he said. "In those days I was workin' aboard the supply ships, delivering essentials all around the land. The Dream Stealers, not wantin' supplies to get through, took to knockin' ships out of the sky. That's what happened. Knocked me straight into the Eternal Forest. When I woke up"—he punched his leg—"I couldn't feel nothin'."

"I'm sorry," said Granny.

"Sorry?" he said, chuckling. "Far as I know, it wasn't you who sent me down, so you got nothin' to be sorry for."

He looked around for the first time, his scored and leathery face unreadable. "Why'd they take your friend?" he asked.

"I don't know."

"That so?" said Sundown, turning back toward the windscreen. "So it's nothin' to do with the fact he's a Knight? And an important one at that."

"How did you know?" Granny said.

"Because only Knights are brave enough—or stupid enough—to go lookin' for Dream Stealers in a snowstorm," said Sundown. "I've met your kind. I used to smuggle Knights into Dream Stealer territory back in the war. I didn't think there were any of you left."

"There are a few," said Granny.

Sundown frowned. "What did you say your name was?"

"It's Eve Wonder," said Granny.

"Wonder," he said. "I'm sure I've heard that name before—"

BOOM!

Granny was thrown against the windscreen as the camper van lurched to one side. She struggled to pull herself back into the seat.

"What's happening?" screamed Julius.

Cornelius gurgled and moaned.

BOOM!

A huge shockwave swept through *Nightstalker*, and the airship dipped again, spiraling blindly in the storm.

Sundown spun around in his chair, fury in his eyes, and let out a head-splitting yell. "Don't just sit there and wait to be saved, you fools!" he cried. "Someone get back there and man the gun! We're bein' set upon by skywaymen—and they've got cannons!"

He spun the wheel of *Nightstalker* with all of his

strength, and the flying camper van ducked through cloud and blizzard like an oversized bee.

With Cornelius trying not to be sick into his cowboy hat, and Julius looking after him, it was up to Granny to man *Nightstalker*'s gun.

"Sit on the seat by my bunk!" bellowed Sundown. "Pull the lever!"

A wooden seat next to the bed was attached to a spring and a lever. Granny sat on the seat and pulled on the lever. The chair catapulted her upward, and she crash-landed on Sundown's bunk bed. The ceiling above had been cut away and replaced by a swiveling glass lookout, from which a rusty gun poked out. Granny grabbed it and scanned the wintry night sky for skywaymen.

A streak of orange flew past. Granny tried to aim the gun, but the ferocity of the snowstorm and the jiggling of the ship made this nearly impossible.

"Will you try to keep us still for a moment!" she yelled.

"Keep still?!" Sundown exclaimed. "Are you completely set on dyin' tonight, woman? Just start shootin' an' hope for the best."

Granny closed her eyes and squeezed the trigger . . .

Nothing happened.

"What the . . . ?" She squeezed the trigger again and again, harder and harder.

Still nothing.

Then something.

A whistling like the sound of an old kettle filled the air, and the gun began to spark and fizz.

CRACK!

A plume of soot erupted from it, filling *Nightstalker*. Granny fell off the bunk and landed with a thud.

"What the blazes happened?" said Sundown.

"Your gun is broken," said Granny. She stumbled back to the copilot's seat and buckled herself in.

Another cannonball flew across the camper van's nose. Sundown yanked the wheel wildly and pulled on more levers.

"That's it," he yelled. "With no defenses we ain't got a choice. We're goin' into the Dream Plains!"

"Is that . . . wise?" Granny asked calmly as the ship lurched forward.

"Wise?" said Sundown. "Of course it ain't wise! But we got no alternative. Out here we're just sitting ducks, waitin' to be blown apart. The Dream Plains are nearby, and they'll give us a better chance. There are things in there that'll gobble down a ship for breakfast."

"But *we're* in a ship!" said Julius faintly.

"We are that," replied Sundown. "The difference is, you've got me."

He pulled on the wheel, and the ship began to descend.

As the thick cloud gave way, a dark expanse of the land below came into view, peppered here and there with village torches.

Sundown peered into a small upside-down periscope.

"What's that?" Granny asked.

"It's a hindoscope," he answered, pushing buttons manically. "Lets me see what's comin' from behind."

Granny put her own eye to it and almost stopped breathing.

Behind them, the skywaymen were thundering through the night sky in a gigantic armored stagecoach, pulled through the air by six winged horses, each the size of an elephant and forged from raging fire.

"Mr. Sundown," said Granny, "I think you'd better speed up."

"*Nightstalker*'s goin' as fast as she can," he shouted. "We can't . . . Wait. There they are. There be the Dream Plains!"

Granny looked through the windscreen and, for a moment, forgot everything that was happening around her.

"Great Nod!" she whispered.

The Dream Plains rose from the land below in a wall of breathtaking light. The colors in the wall were constantly changing, shifting, and moving in shimmering waves across the sky. Granny felt her eyes fill with tears at the sight. It had been so long since she'd gazed upon their majesty.

"Any of you ever been in there?" asked Sundown, breaking the awed silence.

"Once or twice," said Granny. "But only on the ground."

All the Knights had traveled into the Dream Plains as part of their duty, but never in an airship. The skies above this place were as foreign to them as an undiscovered country.

"Well," growled Sundown quietly, "you've been warned. The Dream Plains might take your breath away, but they're full of danger. There are creatures in there that have only just started existin', monsters conjured up from the minds of Wakelings."

Another cannonball screamed past the ship.

"Hang on," Sundown bawled, "we're goin' in!"

He swung the wheel, and the flying camper van swerved, then burst through the wall of light.

26

Rumpous Tinn and Noelle had a problem. The path they'd been following had reached a dead end, and the stream alongside had opened up into a small, deep pool. There seemed to be no way to pass, but Tinn's locator compass insisted they continue on through the wall of rock.

Tinn checked and rechecked the instrument. He spoke to it, shook it, and eventually held it to his ear, listening carefully.

Noelle watched him with interest. "You think the compass is wrong?" she asked, picking up a pebble and throwing it into the water, where it made a satisfying *plunk*.

"It's never been wrong before," replied Tinn.

"So how we gonna get through solid stone?"

Tinn did not answer. He strode over to the dead end and began searching the rock with his hands.

"What're you doing?" asked Noelle.

"There are ways," he answered, "of concealing a doorway, of making it seem invisible." He continued to feel around until every part of the wall had been prodded. "Unfortunately, there is no such doorway here."

"So what do we do?"

"It appears we've hit a brick wall—so to speak," he said thoughtfully.

"Great," moaned Noelle, slumping down. "Just great." She took off her boots and socks, sat down at the water's edge, and dipped her tired toes into the pool.

"Wow!" she exclaimed. "This water's freezing!"

Tinn, who had been staring at the compass again, glanced up. "Of course," he sighed.

"Of course?" said Noelle, squeezing her boots back on. "Of course what?"

"We have to go *in*," replied Tinn, motioning toward the pool.

"In?" she said. "In there? You must be off your rocker. It's like ice!"

Tinn dipped his finger in the water. "It does seem the only way, though, doesn't it?"

Noelle didn't answer. All she could do was stare into the water's depths.

"I'll take a look," said Tinn. "Won't be a tick."

And without a moment's hesitation, the old man jumped into the freezing water.

"He's mental," Noelle whispered to herself, anxiously watching for any sign of him.

Minutes passed.

Nothing.

Noelle began pacing, muttering under her breath.

"Can't believe I got myself mixed up in this. Nutcase . . . Magic compass . . ."

More minutes passed. Still no sign.

Noelle was terrified. No one could hold their breath for that long, could they? A movement in the water caught her eye. At last Tinn bobbed to the surface, where he broke into a little doggy paddle, his long white beard floating in front of him.

"I thought you'd drowned," wailed Noelle.

"Drowned? Nonsense! My dear girl, I've found the entrance. I've found our way out!"

"It's down there?"

"Yes," replied Tinn. "There's a natural underwater passage. It might be rather a long way, though, so you'll need this."

He reached into his beard and produced a pair of little plugs.

"How much stuff do you keep in there?" she asked.

"And what do I do with these?"

"Stick them up your nose."

"I beg your pardon?"

"Just do it, Noelle," he said, adjusting the plugs in his own nostrils. "A Knight should always come prepared for any possibility. These plugs will enable you to breathe underwater for a time."

"A time?" she said slowly. "How long's that, exactly? And what if it ain't long enough to reach the other side?"

"I will not let anything happen to you. Do you trust me?"

She looked into his kindly old face. His eyes twinkled.

"I do," she said. She put in the nose plugs and slipped into the pool.

The icy shock stole her breath, and she could feel the cold water soaking up what little warmth she had left with each passing second.

Tinn's hand gripped her shoulder, and heat radiated through her body. "Are you all right?" he asked.

"I — I'm fine," she managed to stutter. "Let's go. Let's get outta here."

"Very well," he said. "Follow me."

And he disappeared under the rippling surface.

Noelle breathed deeply. Then, taking one last gulp of air, she sank into the swirling cold.

There was a huge explosion. It felt as if the whole world was shaking.

"Why does it feel like we're inside a washing machine?" screamed Zac.

"A what?" said Tilly, hanging on to the lining of her grandfather's coat.

"Never mind."

"That's it," said Tom. "I'm having a look."

"Tom, no!"

It was too late. Zac watched in horror as Tom's beady eyes and mouse whiskers peeked out of the hole in the coat lining. He barely had time to yell, "Wow!" before another thunderous explosion hit the ship.

Cornelius lurched violently in his seat.

"Tilly!" said Zac, as the ship juddered violently. "Are you all right?"

"I'm fine. Where's Tom?"

Zac looked around. Tom was gone.

"He was just there," he said. "He can't have gone far."

Tilly shoved past him and poked her head out. She turned back to Zac, pale and shaken.

"He's out there!" she said. "He's a tiny mouse — he'll be trampled!"

She slipped out through the hole in the coat. Zac hurried after her, landing hard on the deck. He looked down and almost died. There didn't seem to be any floor. He was floating above an endless sea of shimmering color.

"Zac!" Tilly shouted. "It's OK. It's only glass. Come on."

He ran over to where Tilly was sheltering under a tattered seat.

"Where is that idiot?" she said, scanning the shaking airship for her brother.

"Look, just calm down," said Zac. "He must be —"

BANG!

Nightstalker staggered, and they tumbled to their knees.

"Tom!" shrieked Tilly.

Zac looked and saw Tom the mouse lying motionless under Sundown's bunk.

"He's hurt," said Tilly. "Come on."

They tore off across the camper van toward Tom. When they reached him, Tilly put her ear to his furry chest.

"He's alive!"

"Quick, let's get him back into your grandad's coat," said Zac.

They grabbed Tom's mouse tail and began to drag him across the airship. Halfway there, the ship tilted violently and a drawer high above flew open, sending knives and forks the size of lampposts clanging down all around them.

"Speed up!" shrieked Tilly, as a giant knife plunged into the floor only a few inches away.

"I'm trying!" yelled Zac.

"Let go of my tail!" said Tom, who'd come to amid the bedlam.

BOOM!

The van door was ripped open. Cold air roared into the cabin. Julius was catapulted out of his seat belt and came hurtling toward the children.

Instinctively, Zac put his hands up to protect his friends. Something that felt like a shockwave burst from his palms — and Tom and Tilly were miraculously thrown out of harm's way. Zac stared at his fingers for a moment as though they weren't his own. Then he realized Julius was still heading toward him like a moving mountain.

He turned and sprinted, but he was hurled into the air and began skidding backward toward the blown-out door. At the last minute he spotted a loose carpet thread and managed to grab it, but he was traveling so fast that the thread unraveled some distance before it stopped him. He was thrown out of the airship!

Wild, deafening wind whipped at him as *Nightstalker* sliced through the dazzling clouds of the Dream Plains. He was fighting desperately to hold on, but his hands ached and his arm muscles burned. He thought of Granny, of how upset she'd be when she discovered his fate. His grip was failing, and he prepared to fall into the Dream Plains. Were there really dreams unfolding out there among these magical clouds? And were the Dream Stealers out there, too?

The line was yanked suddenly and he found himself being pulled up toward the ship. Another tug brought him closer still, and he gazed up at the straining faces of Tom and Tilly. With one final effort, they heaved Zac up, and he flopped down heavily on the deck of the ship.

They all scampered back into Cornelius's coat.

"You saved my life!" cried Zac, when they were safely inside.

"You saved ours!" said Tom.

BOOM!

"I'm beginning to think we've made a mistake," said Zac.

"What are you talking about?" said Tom, his eyes wide. "That was the most fun I've ever had!"

28

Noelle struggled to keep her bearings in the murky depths. Underwater, the barnacle-covered walls seemed to be closing in. It felt like a watery tomb.

She followed Rumpous Tinn, twisting and turning through cavern after cavern, each one identical to the last. They dived deeper and deeper, and entered another series of caves that took them upward once more. Noelle was becoming increasingly frightened that they were lost, or that she'd run out of air, but it was too late to turn back.

Something brushed against her leg. She stopped and looked around. Nothing. Her heart pounded in her ears. It must have been her imagination. She turned back and began to swim toward Tinn, who was focusing on the compass.

And then she felt the something bite.

Pain shot through her foot and up her leg. It was so intense she thought she might pass out. For a moment, she forgot about Tinn and escaping. She twisted in the icy water in an attempt to see what had caused her agony, and let out a gurgling scream. Deep red clouds of blood were rolling and billowing from a nasty wound on her ankle. Fear filled her mind, weighing her down, and she began to sink . . .

Suddenly a strong hand seized her arm, and Tinn's face came into focus. He'd come back to save her! But his eyes were wide and fearful. She hadn't seen him look frightened before, and that scared her more than anything else. What had he seen? She looked behind.

A creature emerged from the darkness like a train from a tunnel. It looked like a giant octopus — only, instead of tentacles, eight enormous conger eels propelled it through the water. Their terrible bulging eyes were fixed on her, and eight ravenous mouths snapped at the billowing blood. Terror spread through her body like fire.

A fizzing spell flew past her shoulder, briefly stunning the monster. Noelle felt a pull. Tinn was towing her along, swimming much faster than before. She risked another glance behind and was horrified to see that the creature had shaken off the spell and was pursuing them again. They tore through the tunnels as fast as they could kick, up and down, left and right, until Noelle's head was spinning.

The huge octopus was gaining, and the eight eel heads were soon snapping at her heels again. Then, without warning, the eel heads fell back and the enormous body of the creature surged forward.

Let it have given up, thought Noelle. *Please. Just let it go away.*

No such luck. The round body of the creature began to swell, and a gaping mouth appeared, wider than a cave.

Noelle screamed. Little bubbles escaped from her mouth and fizzed away into the icy darkness. The underwater passage began to climb steeply. Tinn strained with every muscle of his body to keep them ahead of the creature's mouth, but it was drawing nearer.

And nearer.

Noelle tucked in her legs, but it was only a matter of time. They were going to be swallowed whole!

The monstrous mouth touched her foot. Soft lips closed around her leg. She could feel herself being sucked inside.

Tinn let loose another spell and again it connected. In a flash, the eight conger eels were gone, replaced by eight tiny puffer fish. Noelle yanked her foot free, and Tinn began to swim again, pulling her along hard in his wake. All at once they surfaced. Noelle felt a rush of cold air against her face.

The old man hoisted himself out.

"Hurry, Noelle," he said, "I can feel the spell won't last more than a few seconds."

She reached for his outstretched hand. Just as Tinn dragged her from the water, the monster erupted from the depths, the eels lunging at her feet again, missing by a hair. She landed hard on the ground as the creature sank back into the pool and out of sight, leaving hundreds of tiny currents and whirlpools on the inky surface.

"What . . . what *was* that?"

"A water demon," said Tinn. "Particularly nasty."

He waved his hand over the wound on her leg, and the flow of blood slowed to a trickle.

They had emerged from the underground stream into a clearing surrounded by thick trees. High above, the moon was shining through the thin clouds. Noelle stared at the sky for a moment, tears filling her eyes. She breathed in deeply. The smell of the forest filled her nostrils, and sweet air rolled over her tongue. She pressed a handful of leaves to her skin.

"We're out," she said softly. "Mr. Tinn, we're out! We

did it!" She threw her arms around him, tears filling her eyes. "Oh, thank you!"

"I never thought —"

Thump!

A large wooden shield spun through the darkness, smashing into Tinn's head. He fell to the ground, scattering a cloud of leaves in the air. Shaking with terror, Noelle instantly became invisible.

Four creatures trudged over to Tinn's prone body. They were all slightly smaller than a grown man, with coarse green skin and oversized eyes that glowed in the dark like a cat's. They were draped in animal skins. The reek stuck in Noelle's throat and a shiver of panic ran through her body.

Goblins.

The largest of the four let out a horrible snort.

"Looks like fresh meat tonight, lads!"

Granny stumbled across the cabin of the camper van and heaved the open door shut.

"That's better!" she said, dropping back into the copilot's chair. "Everyone all right?"

"I think so," said Julius.

"Don't speak to me," said Cornelius into his hat. "I might be sick again."

Granny turned to Sundown. "What happens now?"

"We wait."

The camper van cruised smoothly through the shimmering mist. Granny began to think that without skywaymen, traveling by airship might actually be rather pleasant. She glanced out the passenger window at the kaleidoscope of color outside, and something caught her eye. A huge bird, seemingly made of shimmering smoke, streaked across the sky.

"Would you look at that," she said. "It's an eagle."

"There's another," said Julius, "and another."

The eagles dipped and rolled through the mist, and the sight of them warmed Granny's heart. Then she leaned forward, peering intently, for she thought she'd seen the impossible. Perhaps the shifting clouds were playing tricks with her mind. But no . . . she *had* seen it!

It was a girl. A little girl, soaring with the great birds. Formed from the same smoke as the eagles, she had beautiful wings, and laughed in delight as she spun and twisted and looped.

"It's a dream," said Sundown, and for the first time he gave a real, warm smile. It was as if the sight of such a thing had melted his heart. "That's how Wakelings look when they're dreamin', like spirit and smoke."

"It's beautiful," said Granny.

The eagles and the girl flew nearer. Granny waved to her through the window of the camper van, and the girl twirled in the air. She seemed so happy.

But then her smile disappeared.

"Something's wrong," said Granny. "What's happening to her?"

The girl seemed to be having difficulty staying in the

air. A cloud of inky blackness was forming around her. Feathers began dropping from her wings in great clumps, and the wings themselves seemed unable to support her.

The little girl looked for help, but the eagles had left her. Her desperate gaze met Granny's through the window.

"It's a Dream Stealer," said Sundown sadly. "There's a Dream Stealer down there somewhere, twistin' that poor little girl's dream, plunderin' her fear."

"We have to help her!" cried Granny. As she watched the girl struggle she felt a great ache in her chest.

"There ain't nothin' we can do," said Sundown.

The girl reached out a hand to Granny, who pressed her own hand flat on the glass. And then the little girl was gone, falling through the ocean of color.

"She'll wake up before she lands," said Sundown. "She'll live."

But that didn't matter to Granny. She rested her head on the window and let the tears run down her face. She imagined the little girl waking up at home in the Waking World, scared half to death, knowing that somehow what she'd been through wasn't just a bad dream. Dream Stealers left scars on a Wakeling's mind, and if they got their way, the scars would never heal. It was a harsh reminder of what the Waking World would become if the Dream Stealers were allowed to win.

"Look!" Julius was sitting on the edge of his seat, pointing at the glass window in the floor. His face had turned deathly pale. "There's something else out there," he whispered.

Granny peered into the murk. Was Julius imagining things? But then she saw it, too, and it wasn't the bandit stagecoach; it was something alive, a vast and hideous creature — and they were flying straight toward it.

"What's that?" hissed Granny.

"I don't think it has a name yet," barked Sundown. "I'll wager it's just been brought to life in a dream. The Wakelings have been comin' up with some big, bad stuff since the Dream Stealers resurfaced. We can use it."

Granny peered at him. "Use it? What's that supposed to mean? What are you planning?"

Sundown didn't answer. Throwing the wheel around so that the ship veered sharply to the right, he began to navigate along the monster's enormous length. All they could see were thorny scales the size of trash-can lids.

"What are you doing, Sundown?" she demanded.

He laughed. "Tryin' to keep us alive. I'm looking for this wee beastie's head."

A deep and rumbling roar seemed to rip the air in two.

"Mr. Sundown?" said Julius quietly from the back of the cabin.

"Not now, boy," grunted Sundown.

"But—"

"Not now! Can't you see I'm workin' here?"

"It's just . . . I think I've found the head."

Sundown spun around in his wheelchair and peered at Julius, who pointed toward the glass panel in the floor.

An enormous eyeball stared in at them.

"Well done, boy!" said Sundown. He threw another lever and the camper van lurched forward.

Granny grabbed the hindoscope and searched behind them. "It's following!"

"That's the plan!" said Sundown. "Now, where are those blasted skywaymen? Are they still with us?"

"They're still at the edge of the Dream Plains!" she said. "Two o'clock!"

"Good work."

As the ship swung into position, Granny looked again through the hindoscope and let out a shriek. A massive forked tongue curled around the van.

"I don't think I'll look through that anymore," she said, pushing the instrument away. "Er, Sundown, I take it you have a very good reason to fly back *toward* the skywaymen?"

The skywaymen fired their cannons again, but Sundown didn't flinch. He continued to open up the throttle and steer the shuddering camper van toward them.

Unable to help herself, Granny checked the hindo-scope again.

Behind them was the beast.

In front of them were the bandits.

Neither view was good.

Beast. Skywaymen. Beast. Skywaymen. Beast. Skywaymen.

The beast lunged forward.

Granny screamed.

Sundown wrenched a lever, and *Nightstalker* pulled up sharply.

The beast lumbered past them, unable to stop. The skywaymen tried to swerve out of its path, but there was no time. The monster opened its mouth, swallowing the stagecoach and flaming horses in a single gulp.

"Wooooo-hooooo!" yelled Sundown, punching the air.

Granny looked at the others. Cornelius had almost passed out, and Julius was fanning him with his own hat.

"Well done, Mr. Sundown," she said breathlessly. "Well done indeed."

Sundown laughed heartily. "I told you I was good, didn't I?" he said. "Now, let's get you lot to Port Town."

30

Moonlight reached through the trees and touched the forest floor where the invisible Noelle sat shivering and alone.

After a while, she stood up and shook off her fear like dust. Being scared wasn't going to help her save Mr. Tinn. She had to rescue him. He was her only friend. He'd promised her freedom, and here she was, after a lifetime underground, standing beneath the sky and breathing fresh air. She started after the goblins, down the dirt path winding off into the blackness of the trees.

After a few minutes she smelt a wood fire and spotted dancing flames. The light drew her like a moth. Soon a campsite came into view, and she heard the growling voices of the goblins.

The trees here were enormous, with great knotted trunks perfect for climbing. Noelle shinnied up to the lower branches of one to survey the camp. There were four beds for four goblins. Tinn sat in the center of the camp tied to a tree. He was unconscious.

"You see, fellas?" snorted one goblin. "These little patrols pay off after all, eh?"

"Right you are, Grooble," said another. "We'll eat like kings tonight!"

"That we will," said Grooble. "But before we stuff our bellies, it's time for some shut-eye. Grunge, it's your turn to keep watch. When we wake up, we'll carve up this fella right nice and have us a breakfast to remember!"

The others grunted excitedly, and Noelle watched from her perch as they shuffled off to bed. Within minutes the three were all snoring loudly.

The goblin called Grunge looked greedily at the unconscious Tinn, and took out from his tattered clothing a small piece of wood and a knife. Humming happily to himself, he started to whittle.

A plan began to form in Noelle's head.

She dropped silently from the tree and crept into the camp. She was a master of stealth, and reaching Tinn was easy. He was still out cold. A trickle of dark blood had dried on his face.

Grunge stopped chipping away at his bit of wood and began to sniff at the air. Noelle froze. The goblin set down his little carving and scrambled to his feet, clutching his knife, his nose twitching. He came closer and closer, and his rancid breath began to choke her. She was sure he was going to smell her out! His green eyes flashed.

Then he looked straight at her.

She almost screamed. She knew he couldn't see her, but it was almost as if those enormous eyes were staring directly into her own.

"Oi! Grunge, what you doin'?" Grooble had woken up.

Grunge whirled around. "I . . . thought . . ."

"You don't think, Grunge. Thinkin' gets you in trouble. You're supposed to be *watchin'* the prisoner," said Grooble, settling back to sleep.

"Yeah," said Grunge quietly. "Yeah, right. Sorry, boss." He had one last look, then, to Noelle's relief, he turned away and went back to carving his little piece of wood.

Noelle wiped her brow and took a few deep breaths, steeling herself.

She crouched down behind Tinn. His chest and hands were bound tightly. She could untie him, but it would do no good. They were in full view of the goblins, and even if the stinking creatures somehow failed to notice, she wouldn't be able to carry him. But she had an idea.

She reached down and gently rummaged in his beard, pulling out a length of string, a whistle, and a strawberry sherbet before her hand finally closed around the locator compass. She stowed it in her pocket and stroked the old man's face.

"I'll be back," she whispered, "I promise."

Noelle found it difficult to leave him, but she forced herself to walk away. As she slipped through the camp, she spotted a crate filled with fruit. Stealing a shiny red apple, she cast another look at Tinn and turned back into the forest.

31

Much to Rigby Sundown's great disappointment — and everyone else's great relief — the remainder of the airship journey passed without incident.

Port Town was bathing in the first golden rays of morning sunshine when *Nightstalker* cruised overhead. The harbor was alive with activity. Fleets of fishing vessels were leaving for the far reaches of the Great Lake. Little streets stretched inland in all directions, like the branches of a tree.

They touched down in a small clearing just outside the town. Cornelius was so happy to be back on the ground that he hugged a boulder.

"I'll be here for a few days," said Sundown gruffly.

"I have to fix that blasted broken gun. If I'm still around, an' you're in need of a flight back, I'd be happy to take you. I haven't had such a good time in years!"

"Very kind," said Granny. "We may just take you up on that. Actually, it's rather impressive that the ship is in one piece after what we've just been through."

"This old girl is the toughest bird in the sky," he said, patting the rusty van. A couple of bolts fell to the ground. "Anyway, I hope you find who you're lookin' for. Anyone who stands up to Dream Stealers is all right by me."

He wheeled himself back into the airship.

Cornelius led the way to the harbor front, where a cobbled street wound along the quay.

"Remember, we're looking for an inn called The Grumpy Dragon," he said.

"There it is," said Julius.

The Grumpy Dragon was a run-down shack covered with peeling paint. Dirty water flowed freely from the gutter.

"Lovely," said Granny.

"At least we'll be left alone in there," said Cornelius. "Doesn't look as though it gets many customers."

Inside, a craggy man with an eye patch was sitting behind a cluttered desk reading that day's *Port Town Reporter*. He didn't bother to look up.

Cornelius stood at the desk for a moment.

The man paid no attention.

Cornelius cleared his throat.

Still there was no reaction.

"What about that bell?" said Granny, and she reached over and pressed a button with the word SERVICE engraved upon it.

There was a tinkling noise, and the eye-patch man jumped to attention, smiling falsely. He only had one tooth, and it didn't look as though it would last very much longer.

"How can I be of assistance?" he simpered.

"We'd like two rooms," said Cornelius.

"Of course, sir," said the man in a smarmy tone. "Follow me."

He led them up a dingy staircase to a couple of very shabby rooms. Granny was given one to herself, while Cornelius and Julius shared the other. Eye Patch hung around for a tip, only leaving after Cornelius threw him a few teeth.

"He's a real charmer," said Cornelius when Granny had gone to her room. "Julius, are you all right? You look awfully pale."

Julius was sitting on the edge of his bed, fidgeting. His face was ashen, and he kept looking out the window and jumping whenever there was a noise from the hallway outside.

"I — I'm fine," he said. "Just worn out after that trip. I'm not a big fan of flying."

"Well, that makes two of us," said Cornelius, taking off his coat and draping it over the end of the bottom bunk. "We'd better get some rest. Gideon should be here with some news soon."

At the mention of Gideon's name, Julius's face turned even paler.

Zac, Tom, and Tilly climbed out of Cornelius's fur coat and onto the dusty floor. High above, Cornelius was snoring loudly on the bed.

"Wow!" said Tom, his whiskers twitching madly. "That was unbelievable! Brilliant!"

"*Brilliant?*" said Tilly in disbelief. "We almost got killed, you idiot."

"Yeah," said Tom. "How good was that! Skywaymen, Tilly! Real skywaymen! And a monster the size of a hundred dragons!"

"I need some air," said Zac. "No offense, but your grandad's coat isn't the nicest place to get stuck for a night."

Tilly and Tom agreed, and soon they were scurrying back down the stairs of the inn.

They had just reached the hallway when they heard footsteps descending the stairs behind them. They squeezed themselves into a dusty corner.

It was Julius.

"Where's he going?" Zac whispered.

Julius opened the door, looked over his shoulder, and disappeared into the street.

"He's up to no good," said Tom. "Let's follow him."

But before they could move, the door swung open again, and three burly figures came striding in, followed by a fourth. The first three were men, all tall and powerfully built. The fourth was a woman, dressed in gray.

Zac felt his insides contract. "I think this is the trap!" he spat. "You were right about Julius—he's led Granny and the Knights here to be killed!"

Tom's face flooded with fear.

The woman in gray approached the desk and whispered something inaudible to the innkeeper. Eye Patch stared up at her, his one eye wide with fright. He pointed to the stairs.

"We have to do something," said Tilly, her hands clutching her face.

The woman had begun to lead the group up the stairs.

"C'mon," said Tom. "Quick!"

Tilly and Zac leapt onto his back, and they quickly overtook the four ominous figures. Tom scampered along the corridor and they squeezed under the door to Cornelius's room. The old man was fast asleep.

Reaching into his pocket, Zac quickly pulled out the bottle of growth serum. He looked at the others.

"Here goes!" he said. He popped open the bottle and let two electric blue drops fall onto his tongue, then he tossed the rest to Tilly. The liquid was sweeter than syrup. With a loud *ZING*, Zac was back to his normal size. A moment later, he heard another *ZING* and Tilly appeared beside him.

Tom changed himself back to his human form and made for the bed.

"Grandad! Wake up!" he said, shaking the old man.

Cornelius's eyes shot open and he leapt from the bed, throwing frantic, clumsy karate chops at Tom, who backed away into the corner, shielding his face.

"Grandad, it's me! It's Tom, you loon!"

Cornelius froze mid-chop. His eyes flicked between the three children.

"Tilly? Tom? Zac? What the . . . how?" His face began to grow red with anger.

"Grandad, there's no time!" Tom said urgently. "There are people coming up the stairs. We think they're Dream Stealers here to kill you!"

"Are you sure?" he whispered, combing his mustache into place with his fingertips.

"Pretty much."

Cornelius looked around the room. "Where's Julius?"

"He ran away," said Tom. "We saw him. He's the one who led them here."

"I have to get to Granny," said Zac.

He made for the door, but Cornelius pulled him back.

"Too dangerous, boy," he whispered.

Zac was about to argue, but the door was thrown open and the three men rushed in.

Cornelius jumped to his feet and hurled a jinx at the first. It met its mark, and the man fell to the floor — with a growl.

"What's happening to him?" yelled Zac.

The man was changing before their eyes. His skin was bubbling and stretching, and hair was sprouting everywhere. His face elongated into a snout. Huge teeth erupted in his mouth, and great muscled arms and legs tore holes in his clothes.

"That's not a Dream Stealer!" said Tom. "That's a . . ."

"Werewolf!" Zac finished.

The monster howled, and Zac covered his ears. The other two men had also begun their hideous transformations. In a matter of moments, three huge and angry beasts were eyeballing them.

Cornelius caught the nearest werewolf with a well-aimed spell, turning its feet into a knot of matted fur. It toppled back into the corridor with a howl.

The two remaining creatures circled the children.

"Zac!" cried Tom from across the room. "The silver dagger!"

Zac reached into his cloak.

"Quick!" said Tom. "Give it to Tilly!"

Confused, Zac did as he was told.

The pair of werewolves growled and drew themselves up to their full height before rushing forward in attack. But suddenly, Tilly was in front of Zac, shielding him, every inch of her gleaming. By touching the dagger, she'd turned to silver — and there was nothing werewolves hated more.

The first werewolf collided with her and howled in pain. The second flew toward Tom, but he shrank back into a mouse, and it smashed through the window behind him and down into the alleyway outside.

Zac heard a crash from the next room.

Granny!

Zac sprinted into the shabby corridor, where Cornelius was fighting off the third creature, which had freed its feet from the matted fur. One of the magician's flashing spells missed its target, and, as Zac flew past, a crater appeared in the wall above his head. Images from his dream spun through his mind. It was becoming real. Then he remembered the part where Granny was begging for help. He felt ill with fear.

Granny's door had been blown from its hinges. Zac stepped cautiously into the room. One of the beds was broken in half and the window shattered. A yellow-eyed werewolf the size of a bear stood over Granny, who had fallen to her knees in the corner.

"Granny!"

Eve saw her grandson and her eyes widened in horror. She reached out an arm.

"Zac, run!"

At that moment, the werewolf lashed out and struck her with a blow so devastating that she was unconscious before her head hit the floor. Zac let out a guttural scream.

The werewolf turned, steaming mucus dripping from its muzzle. With a terrifying howl, it charged. Zac tried to stay calm. If only he *could* do magic, if only he had some sort of ability. With furious concentration, he pictured a shockwave erupting from his hands. He threw out his arm, pointed, and . . .

Nothing happened.

The werewolf hit him in the chest like a rocket, and he was thrown against the crumbling wall. He slid down into a heap, the salty taste of his own blood filling his mouth.

Sensing victory, the werewolf moved back to Granny.

"Get away from her!"

A familiar voice rang in Zac's ears.

From nowhere, a tall stick figure leapt over Zac and strode toward Granny, a flashing spell knocking the werewolf back against the wall.

It was Gideon!

The werewolf circled him, its low growl intensifying into a howl, and went straight for Gideon's throat. But the Knight was too fast. He threw out his hand and entangled the werewolf in a magical web. Then, drawing a miniature crossbow from his coat, he fired a silver arrow at its heart. The werewolf exploded in a cloud of smoke and glowing cinder.

Gideon lifted Granny from the floor, and offered Zac a hand.

"Are you all right?" he said.

"I think so."

Cornelius appeared at the door with Tom and Tilly. "The other werewolves have scarpered," he said breathlessly.

"They won't be back," replied Gideon. "I've taken care of their leader. Now, would someone care to tell me what in Nocturne is going on?"

32

"Will she be all right?" asked Zac as Gideon lay Granny gently down on the bed in the mangled room.

"She'll be fine," said Gideon. "Thankfully, the werewolf didn't bite. If it had, she'd be in deep trouble. She'll wake up soon with a headache, that's all."

There was a scratching noise from the door, and they all turned to see Eye Patch. He swayed on the spot.

"Look at the state of this place!" he barked. "There are holes in the walls, broken-down doors . . . that'll be extra, you know."

Gideon flew across the room and pinned the innkeeper to the wall. "Listen to me, dung-licker," he said. "If you are *very* lucky, I won't hold you responsible for endangering the lives of my friends. Now, you will go back downstairs and you will lock the front door. If you let anyone else into this building, I'll make sure that it's nothing more than a pile of stinking rubble before I leave. Understand?"

The innkeeper's one eye bulged. He nodded. Gideon released his grip and watched him scramble away, then he turned coolly to the others.

"So, what's been going on?" he asked.

Cornelius began to update Gideon on everything that he'd missed, including the attack on Mrs. Huggins and the fact that the Dream Stealers now had one of the locator compasses.

"And Zac keeps having dreams that come true," added Tilly. "He knew Eve was in danger."

"You had a dream, Zac?" asked Cornelius. "Here in Nocturne?"

Zac's stomach did a horrible flip. Everyone was staring at him again.

"That's why we stowed away," said Tom. "We knew Julius was double-crossing you, and we wanted to help."

Cornelius smiled kindly. "Well, I for one am very glad you did," he said. "But how *did* you know it was Julius?"

Tilly and Tom looked at the floor. "We . . . we over-heard Gideon accusing him of being a spy," mumbled Tilly. "When we were sneaking around HQ."

Gideon stared at them. "It's true," he said at last. "I did suspect him—have for weeks. He's been different . . . on edge all the time. I even caught him breaking into Tinn's quarters. He denied he was up to anything sinister, of course. I was watching the inn when you arrived this morning. I wanted to make sure that Julius wasn't leading you into a trap. Unfortunately, I was right to doubt him. No sooner had you arrived than he snuck out like a rat. The werewolves were already waiting outside. Julius said something to them, and then he disappeared off down an alley. That's when the werewolves stormed in here and tried to make breakfast out of you."

Cornelius buried his head in his hands. "How could Julius be capable of such madness?" he moaned.

Granny's voice came unexpectedly from the back of the room. "More powerful magicians than Julius have been turned by dark magic," she managed weakly.

"Granny!"

She was sitting up, blinking away the cobwebs. Zac felt like flying. He hugged her tightly.

"I'm all right, lad," she said. "It'll take more than a bop on the head to stop your old granny. The question in my mind now is: Where do we go from here? How do we find Tinn with a traitor one step ahead of us? We don't even have the unfinished compass anymore. I'm afraid we're at a dead end—unless you've been able to dig up something, Gideon?"

Her savior sat at the foot of the bed and removed his top hat.

"As a matter of fact," he began, "I did have a bit of luck with the old ship captain I was telling you about at breakfast yesterday. I met him in a tavern a few streets away. Turned out he was rather fond of Dragon Brandy. After we'd shared a bottle, he was ready to tell me anything."

"And?" said Granny.

"And . . . he took his ship up toward the Northern Mountains a few months ago. It's pretty remote up there. Not many ships make the journey. They got so far and found that a section of river had been blocked. There was a village nearby, so they stopped to investigate. Half of his crew left the ship. That's when he heard the screams. All he could tell me was that he saw his men being ripped apart by screeching shadows. He and the rest of his crew turned the ship around and fled."

"Vampires," breathed Granny.

"Sounds that way," said Cornelius. "How terrible."

"This could be useful, though," Granny added.

"What do you mean?" asked Zac.

"If there's anyone in Nocturne who knows where the Dream Stealers are holed up, it'll be the vampires."

"What do you suggest, Eve?" Cornelius quizzed.

"We head to the village in question," said Granny. "If we can capture one of those vampires, we might be able to persuade it to tell us where the Dream Stealers could be hiding Tinn."

"It's certainly worth a try," Cornelius said, cracking his knuckles so loudly that Zac flinched. "But we'll need a way of getting there."

"I can help there," said Gideon. He stood up and popped his top hat back on. "I know a few more captains down at the harbor. I'm sure one of them'll be willing to risk their neck—providing we dangle enough teeth in front of them. Shouldn't take more than an hour or two to sort something out."

"Smashing," said Granny. "Good work, Gideon. Get back as soon as you can."

Without another word, Gideon nodded and strode out of the room.

"Granny," said Zac, "are we *seriously* going to walk straight into a village full of vampires?"

Granny tutted. "Give us a little credit, lad," she said. "The vampires won't even know we're there."

33

Noelle sat at the edge of the swirling stream, warming her bones by the fire she'd built and crunching into the apple she'd snatched from the goblin camp. She'd known how to build a fire ever since she was little. There had been a prisoner who'd taught her, a kind man called Joseph who'd been walking in the Northern Mountains and had stumbled upon the Dream Stealers. She remembered how he'd changed . . . how he had wasted away. At the beginning, he'd been strong as an ox, and when he laughed at her jokes the whole room seemed to shake. In the end, though, he'd faded to skin and bone, and the last time she snuck in food for him, he didn't even know who she was.

She wiped the tears from her eyes and spun the locator compass in her hands, watching firelight sparkle in its casing. Would it work for her? Tinn had said he was the only one who could use it.

She popped open the lid. She might as well give it a try.

"Please," she whispered. "Please, I need you to show me the way to save Mr. Tinn."

She started in surprise as the instrument whirred to life. The little dial spun faster and faster. When it stopped, it pointed directly at the water. Noelle stared into the dark, freezing depths.

"No," she said. "We've only just escaped from there. I ain't goin' back. How's that gonna help Mr. Tinn?"

She shook the compass hard.

It clearly wasn't working for her.

She held it still once again and inhaled deeply. She'd give it one more go.

"Please," she pleaded. "I've gotta help Mr. Tinn. Show me how."

Once more the dial whizzed around. Faster and faster it spun until, again, the needle came to rest pointing at the water.

Noelle sighed and threw the compass to the ground in despair. It was no good. Only Mr. Tinn could work it and he was otherwise engaged with some rather fearsome goblins.

She sat with her head in her hands until, from nowhere, a thought struck her. She glanced down at the compass through narrowed eyes, and then shifted her gaze to the water. She couldn't help laughing at the cleverness of the idea.

Of course! The compass *was* working. It was working better than ever! And it was telling her exactly what to do. She stood up and snatched it from the ground, wiping the dust from its copper casing. She gave it a kiss for luck and stuffed it back into her clothes, then took one last bite of her apple and tossed it into the pool. No sooner had the apple core hit the water than there was a great rush of churning bubbles. The hideous water demon had been waiting, ready to pounce, if anyone were to venture too close. It snatched the core and disappeared back into the depths.

The trap was set.

Noelle rushed back down along the path to the goblin camp. Three of the goblins were still asleep, and Grunge was still occupied by his carving.

For a moment, Noelle stood on the edge of the camp, contemplating the wisdom of what she was about to do. Then she made herself visible.

"Excuse me," she said.

Grunge snorted in shock and looked up from his carving. When his large green eyes met hers, he dropped his piece of wood into the fire. He didn't say anything; he simply sat there and stared.

"I was just wondering," continued Noelle, "if you're planning on ever letting my friend go?"

Still the goblin said nothing.

"Because if you ain't," she continued, "then I'm afraid I'm gonna have to take him from you. It's nothing personal."

Grunge slowly stood up. "Boss?" he said loudly. "Mr. Grooble, wake up!"

The other goblins stirred from their slumber, groaning loudly.

"You better have a bloody good reason for waking me up, Grunge," burbled Grooble.

"You bet your life I do, boss. We got ourselves another visitor."

Grooble's gaze locked onto Noelle. He sprang to his feet. The others followed, licking their lips.

"She says she's here," continued Grunge with a grin, "to rescue the old man."

"Is that so?" Grooble smirked.

"Mm-hmm," said Noelle sweetly. "He's my friend."

Grooble laughed wickedly. "Well, my pretty," he said, "I hate to disappoint you, but that old man ain't goin' nowhere — except in here."

He pointed to his large belly and snorted. The others laughed in appreciation.

"Human meat don't stroll into our camp too often, see," he continued, smacking his lips. "An' when it does, we don't let it go to waste."

Noelle's heart was beating so fast it felt like a hummingbird in her chest.

Wait for it, she thought. *Just wait*.

"Now, you appearing here has presented us with a bit of a dilemma," said Grooble. "See, now I ain't sure who we should eat first—him or you."

Noelle turned and ran. She tore up the path to the stream, the heavy footsteps of the goblins crashing behind her.

She didn't look back; she didn't dare because she knew they were close. The pool came into view ahead. She readied herself. When she reached the water's edge, she turned to face the oncoming rabble.

"Grab her!" yelled Grooble.

Noelle waited until they were almost upon her—and then she disappeared.

Grooble's momentum almost carried him over the edge, but he managed to halt in the nick of time. Seconds later, the others crashed into the back of him, and they all tumbled into the pool, their gruesome faces twisted in confusion.

All except for one.

Grunge stood swaying on the edge, his orb-like eyes wide and his arms flailing. Noelle took instant action. She pushed him in with everything she had.

Grunge let out a squeal as he too fell into the icy water.

All four goblins were coughing and spluttering. Then one disappeared.

Then another.

And another and another.

There were waving limbs and screams of agony as the goblins were devoured by the water demon. The monster's eely tentacles seemed to be everywhere, writhing and snapping, the water turning crimson.

After a time, all became quiet and still. Noelle stumbled away, heading back toward the goblin camp and Rumpous Tinn.

34

It was barely noon when the Knights set off up the river from Port Town, but already darkness was creeping across the northern skies.

"They only get a few hours of sunlight here each day," said Granny. "That's why vampires live in the North. They do most of their hunting in the dark."

Gideon had succeeded in finding a captain who was willing to take them close to the vampire village, although the Knights had handed over quite a few teeth to secure her services. Her name was Lila Muldoon, and she was remarkable for two reasons. The first was that she was the only captain in the entire North who happened to be a woman. The second was that her ship wasn't really a ship at all. It was a gigantic, twisted oak tree that stood in the river and moved through the water using its roots, which grabbed the riverbed like great fingers.

The cabin was a two-story tree house nestled in the upper branches. From there, Zac could see out over the Eternal Forest lining the river, all the way to the Northern Mountains.

A few hours into the journey, it had grown completely dark. The moon shone in the night sky, a shiny new coin on a black velvet cushion.

As her crew hummed around the tree like worker bees, Lila Muldoon entertained the Knights with tales of her travels all over Nocturne. Tall and beautiful, with flawless dark skin and a head of short, tight black curls, her brown eyes twinkled as she spoke of her adventures. Zac liked her straightaway.

"There ain't a corner of the known land I'm yet to see," she boasted. Then a dreamy look swept over her face. "But the Eternal Forest, that's a whole different bag of fish guts. They say it goes on forever. I'm gonna find out one day . . ."

Lila's cook served up steaming fish stew from the galley, and Zac gobbled it down—even the squirming pink tentacles that were trying to escape the wooden bowl.

"Granny," he said quietly as the others chatted

amongst themselves, "are you angry with me for stowing away with Tom and Tilly?"

Granny gave him a sideways glance and smiled crookedly. "I'm not angry, lad," she said. "How could I be? You helped save our lives. And by the way, those shrinking pills were a brilliant idea!" She ruffled his messy hair.

Zac was eager to ask Granny about the dreams he'd been having, but before he could speak, Lila Muldoon appeared again, looking much more serious than before.

"We're almost there," she said. "The vampire village is half a mile upriver. I've talked to the crew, and we ain't willin' to go any farther. We'll sort you out with transport the rest of the way."

"We understand," said Granny. "And we're grateful you were willing to take us this far."

"What you plannin' to do when you get there?" Lila asked.

The Knights looked at one another.

"We're going to capture a vampire," said Gideon.

Lila's eyes narrowed. "Look, you might not have told me so, but it's obvious to me that you're Knights," she said. "I know you got strong magic. But we're talkin' about vampires here. A *lot* of vampires, from what I've heard. They say even the goblins don't like goin' near — unless they're on the trail of food."

"Thank you for the warning, Lila," said Granny. "But

we have no choice. One of our friends needs help — and the vampires know where he is."

Lila led the Knights out to the upper tree, and they climbed down a series of ladders until they'd reached the lower branches. Two crewmen appeared, carrying the largest leaf Zac had ever seen. It was as big as a car. Lila expertly tied a line to it and the crewmen tossed it into the water.

"The flow of the river'll take you as far as you need to go," said Lila. "You'll see the village soon enough. Good luck to you. I hope we meet again."

She turned and climbed back up the tree toward the cabin. The crewmen threw a rope ladder down to the giant floating leaf, and Zac and the others shinnied down and climbed aboard. Then the crewmen cut them loose, and they began drifting away from the tree-ship. As they rounded a corner, Zac saw Lila watching from the upper branches until they were out of sight.

The river moved them quickly. In a few minutes, the trees on one side of the water began to clear, and the vampire village came into view. Even in the darkness, Zac could see that most of the houses were crumbling wrecks, covered in creeping plants and moss.

Granny leaned over the side of the leaf and aimed her little spectacle-arm wand at the water. The waves changed direction, and began pushing the boat to the shore. When they reached the bank, the Knights climbed out of the vessel and huddled together.

"Well," said Gideon, "this is it."

"We'll cover the village more quickly if we split into teams," said Granny. "Zac will stick with me. Cornelius, you take Tom and Tilly. Gideon, I'm afraid that means you're on your own. Now, chances are, most of the vampires'll be out hunting, so we might be lucky enough to find one alone. Meet back here in ten minutes to report."

The others nodded and headed off into the gloom. Tom and Tilly gave Zac an excited wave before they disappeared.

As he followed Granny, Zac had to fight off the urge to be sick. Here they were in a village in the middle of nowhere, probably surrounded by dozens of vampires, all of whom would love nothing more than to suck out his blood.

"What happens if we're discovered?" he whispered as they crept into a narrow street.

"You'll run back to the boat and get as far away as possible," said Granny. "I'll distract them."

"But—"

Granny held up a finger to silence him. Something creaked above. Suddenly, the sound of flapping wings echoed through the cold air. Granny grabbed Zac and pulled him behind an abandoned cart. Zac's blood thundered through his veins. He glanced up and saw a few crows disappearing into the black sky. He let out a sigh of relief.

"Thank the stars," whispered Granny. "I thought we'd been busted!"

Zac stared at her in disbelief. She was smiling! She was actually enjoying herself.

They crawled out from behind the cart and crept down the street, carefully checking the abandoned houses. Zac saw no trace of life anywhere. If there were vampires here, then they were very well hidden. Maybe Granny was right, and they were all out hunting. He began to hope the stories had been wrong and the vampires had never been here at all.

They heard the cry as they turned another corner. Something was lying on the road up ahead. Granny stepped in front of Zac and edged closer.

"Gideon!" she breathed. She knelt down and rolled him over. There was a cut on his forehead. His eyes blinked open.

"Mrs. Wonder," he said. "I don't know what happened. Something flew out from the shadows and hit me."

As Granny helped him up, they heard a terrible scream. It was a chilling noise, as if someone were literally being scared to death.

"Come on!" gasped Gideon. "We must help."

As they pounded the streets, the screams continued. Zac began to imagine horrible things happening to his friends. They tore around a corner, and ran straight into Cornelius, Tom, and Tilly.

"Thank the stars you're all right!" said Granny over the shrieks.

"We thought it was *you* making that racket," stammered Cornelius.

Another desperate cry ripped through the dark.

"Well, someone's in trouble," said Gideon. "We have to help."

Led by Granny, the Knights followed the tortured sounds through the winding streets until they reached the source.

"In there," said Cornelius, pointing to what must have been an impressive mansion once, but was now, like the rest of the village, a crumbling shell. The door was ajar. Granny pushed it open just as the loudest scream yet made them all jump.

"Sounds like they're ripping someone apart in here," whispered Gideon.

Her wand drawn, Granny led the way into a yawning entrance hall. Huge cobwebs covered almost everything. The air smelt damp and musty. Zac thought he saw streaks of blood on the wall. They reached a narrow staircase leading down into a cellar. Another shriek of pain erupted from below.

They crept down the stairs. The darkness here was so thick that Cornelius had to light the way with a magical fireball. At the bottom, they found a suffocating stone corridor leading to an open door.

In the room beyond, an old woman faced them on her knees. She was bound to the wall by heavy chains. When she spotted them, she reached out desperately.

"Please!"

"Come on," said Granny, and they rushed into the room. Cornelius shot a spell at the chains, and they burst from the wall in a shower of sparks. Granny helped the withered old woman to her feet.

"Listen!" said Zac.

Footsteps echoed down the staircase and along the corridor. Zac was so frightened he couldn't breathe. A man appeared in the doorway. He was tall and broad, with cropped silver hair, and he wore a bloodred cloak.

Then Zac heard laughter. Everyone stared at the old woman. She was cackling quite madly. She broke free of Granny's grasp and joined the man at the door.

"Thank you, Esme," he said in a voice like melted chocolate. "Now, go and fetch the others."

Stunned, Zac and the Knights stared after the hag

as she disappeared down the corridor, still laughing wickedly.

"What's going on?" demanded Cornelius. "Who are you?"

The man with the silver hair closed the door.

"My name is Raven," he said smoothly. "I am very glad you have finally arrived. I've been so looking forward to tasting your blood."

35

"I am growing a little tired of waking up with a headache," said Tinn as Noelle untied him. He felt the bruise on his head. "Where are those goblins now?"

Noelle looked nervously at him. She produced the locator compass from her pocket. "I hope you ain't mad," she said, "but I had to take it. I know you said you were the only one who could use it, but when they snatched you I didn't know what else I could do. So I snuck in and took it. I asked it how to rescue you. And it told me, Mr. Tinn! It worked! The compass told me to lead the goblins to the water, so that's just what I did, and they got eaten by the same demon that tried to have us for dinner!"

Tinn stared at her for a moment, then held out his hand. Noelle dutifully placed the compass back in his palm. He smiled proudly at her.

"Well I never," he said. "You're a bit of a surprise, aren't you? Thank you, Noelle. Thank you for helping me."

"Well," she began thoughtfully, "I reckoned you'd do the same for me. I only wish I had more magic like yours."

Tinn smiled. "Well, you do very well with your gift of invisibility," he said. "And now you've shown you're special enough to work my compass, who knows what other talents we might uncover?"

"Yeah, but it must be great, having real magic powers. If I had magic like you've got, I'd have turned those goblins into slimy slugs and that would have been that."

"It's not quite that simple," chuckled Tinn. "Magic is not always the answer."

"Why not? It seems pretty useful to me."

"Well, you see, magic spills out from the Dream Plains — that's where it comes from — and it's shaped by imagination. To perform a spell correctly, you must have a clear picture in your head of what you want it to do. It requires extreme concentration, and it is unpredictable. It also saps your energy very quickly."

Noelle arched her eyebrows. "Do you think I can do more, though? I mean, do you think I can do other magic as well as becoming invisible?"

"I think you have only begun to discover your magical talent," said Tinn. "Although you would do well to remember that Knights judge others on how they choose to use their power, not by how much power they possess."

"Will you teach me?" she said.

Tinn did not answer. He stood up and studied the dense forest surrounding them.

"Perhaps we need a little more light," he said.

He clicked his fingers, and Noelle stumbled back, shielding her eyes from the dazzling fireball that had appeared in his hand.

"Ah, effective, isn't it? Now the way to create fire is —"

Thwack.

"What was that?" said Noelle. She peered at the ground, leaned over, and dislodged a large arrow from the earth.

Thwack, thwack, thwack! Thwack!

Four more arrows were now lodged in the ground at their feet.

Noelle looked up. She screamed.

Dozens of pairs of huge green eyes were staring down at them from among the branches, all reflecting the fire in Tinn's hand.

"A goblin mob!" she said. "What do we do?"

Thwack! Thwick-thwick! Thwack!

Tinn pulled the locator compass from his beard again. "We ask for an escape route. Follow me!"

36

Zac shot a sideways glance at Granny. She hurriedly reattached her wand to her glasses, concealing it from the vampire.

"When you say you've been looking forward to tasting our blood, you mean to say that you've been expecting us?" she said.

Raven smiled, and Zac caught a glimpse of a huge set of fangs. He looked at Tom, who stared back, terrified.

"I was expecting only you, Mrs. Wonder," said Raven. "The werewolves were meant to dispose of your friends in Port Town. No matter. I'll be happy to finish the job."

"And what do you intend to do with me?" pressed Granny.

"A group of Dream Stealers arrived in the village this morning to collect you. I'll let them explain that to you."

"What about us?" said Tom.

Raven flashed his fangs again. "Well, I'm sure you'll all be delicious."

Tilly shrieked. Zac felt his throat closing over in fear.

Without warning, Cornelius lifted his arm and shot at Raven with a burst of magical fire, but the vampire vanished in a wisp of red mist and the spell hit the wall, leaving a scorching crack in the stone. Instantly, Raven reappeared, striking Cornelius across the face with the back of his hand, and the old man tumbled to his knees.

"The next person who tries anything like that will be dead before they hit the floor," the vampire spat.

More footsteps echoed outside in the passage, and someone rapped on the door.

"Come," said Raven, and the door swung open.

Zac gasped.

Four figures strode in, all cloaked in black. Their faces were hidden beneath terrifying silver skull masks, and their silver-plated arms crossed their chests. He'd seen an identical figure in the last dream he'd had in the Waking World!

Granny reached her arm around his shoulder and peered at him over her glasses. "It's OK, Zac," she said softly.

She made to step forward.

"Oh, I wouldn't try anything stupid," said Raven. "I'm just dying for an excuse to spill the blood of one of these children. Delectable, you know?"

He glanced hungrily at Zac, whose stomach did a somersault.

Tom and Tilly stepped protectively in front of him.

"How touching," sneered Raven.

"Tom! Tilly! Stay still!" Cornelius yelled. "That's an order!"

Raven rolled his eyes. "Let's just get this over with, shall we?" he said. "This is Twist. He will escort you."

He gestured to the tallest of the Dream Stealers, who stepped forward, removing his hideous mask to reveal a twisted face with lopsided eyes and a crooked nose.

"Mrs. Wonder," said the lopsided man with a phony smile, "you will come with us. The leader of the Dream Stealers would very much like to meet you. She's gone to a lot of trouble to see that you end up here." Then he turned his shifty eyes to Raven. "The rest are yours to pick at as you please."

Zac looked at Granny, horror-struck. They couldn't take her away!

"I'll die before I leave my grandson," said Granny stoutly.

"Mrs. Wonder, you are outmatched and outnumbered. We will remove you by force if we must."

The other Dream Stealers stepped forward.

"Let me see," said Granny, "there are six of us, four of you, and quite possibly dozens of vampires." She shrugged. "I like our chances."

Twist laughed. "I admire your courage, Mrs. Wonder, but you should count again. There are only five of you."

Granny shot him a puzzled look. "What are you talking about?"

The Dream Stealer reached into his cloak, pulled out a large velvet bag, and tossed it across the room. It arched, just missing the ceiling, and fell neatly into the bony hands of Gideon Small. Gideon untied the end of the bag and looked inside.

"It's all there," said Twist. "Five thousand teeth."

Gideon nodded, ignoring the stunned faces of Cornelius, Granny, and the children, and took his place behind the Dream Stealers.

"Gideon," said Cornelius, his eyes wide. "What's this?"

Twist snickered. "There are only five of you," he said, "because *he* is with *us*."

37

Noelle ran as fast as she could through the labyrinthine forest. Tinn was ahead, taking care every now and then to check the locator compass. They'd made so many twists and turns that Noelle was beginning to wonder if they were going in circles.

"This way," shouted Tinn. He swung past a tree and headed up a steep slope, turning briefly to check on Noelle and what might be behind in the darkness. For a fleeting moment, fear clouded his face, then he composed himself.

"Noelle," he said, "whatever you do, don't look back."

After being warned explicitly not to do something,

Noelle did what everyone else in the entire universe would do: exactly the opposite.

She immediately regretted it.

The goblin horde was gaining, panting like ravenous dogs, their eyes shining through the blackness like beacons of evil.

And then Noelle noticed something else, and terror gripped every part of her.

Some of them were wearing human skins.

She'd heard stories about how goblins liked to keep the skins of their human victims as trophies. Her stomach heaved, and though her lungs burned and her legs ached, she forced herself to run faster.

Thwack!

Something walloped violently into a tree beside her.

"More arrows!" she said. "Mr. Tinn! They're firing at us again."

Thwack, thwack, thwack!

Three arrows narrowly missed her.

Tinn, a few paces ahead, wheeled around, the fireball in his hand reflected in his eyes.

"What're you doin'?" screamed Noelle. "They'll catch you!"

"Keep running!" said Tinn.

Noelle passed the old man, who headed back toward their pursuers. Arrows rained down on him as he walked, but none seemed to find their mark. Noelle slowed. A choking feeling rose in her throat. She couldn't leave him. She stayed rooted to the spot as Tinn stood his ground.

He threw his hands in the air, and Noelle felt the wind pick up in answer to his spell. It whistled through the trees, and the fallen leaves at her feet began to swirl. As the leaves blew in the air, they gathered together, forming a huge shape — the shape of a man! Tinn had conjured up a giant, and now he stood at its feet, the wind whipping through his beard. As the goblins approached, Tinn pointed forward, and the leaf man began to charge, thundering through the darkness.

The giant collided with the horde. Leaves flew and goblins screamed.

Tinn dropped to his knees. Noelle ran to him and helped him stand.

"You OK?" she asked.

"I'm fine," replied Tinn breathlessly. "But there's no time for talking. We have only seconds before —"

Thwack!

From nowhere, an arrow plunged into the old man's back.

Noelle screamed in horror as Tinn slumped against her, shock etched into the deep lines of his face. They fell to the ground together.

"Mr. Tinn! Oh, Mr. Tinn."

"Run," he whispered. "Take the locator compass . . . it will lead you out of goblin country."

Hot, stinging tears filled Noelle's eyes, and she could taste them as they ran down her face. He couldn't die. Not now. She looked sternly at him.

"I ain't leaving you," she said. "No way. We got this far together, and we're gonna get out together."

She wrapped his arm around her shoulder and heaved, struggling under his weight.

"Noelle," he said, "I don't know how far I can go."

"Just a little farther, Mr. Tinn, I can feel it. Come on, I'll help you."

She glanced at the arrow sticking out from his shoulder. A spreading bloodstain soaked his white robes.

"Shouldn't we pull that out?" she asked.

"We don't have time," Tinn said. "Let's get moving. We can take care of that later." He sparked another fireball in his hand, but this one was much smaller and dimmer than before, and it only partially lit the way. When they reached another clearing in the forest, they stopped to catch their breath. A thick layer of cloud lay heavily across the sky.

"Which way?" said Noelle.

"The compass," wheezed Tinn. "Here, ask it."

He thrust the small copper instrument into her hand.

"Which way to escape?" she asked. The little dial

pointed straight ahead. Noelle looked at Tinn. She knew that he wanted her to take the compass and run, but she still gave it back. They began to move again.

"Noelle," he said, struggling for breath, "thank you."

She smiled kindly at him. "You know, Mr. Tinn, it's strange, but I reckon I was meant to meet you."

"Really?" said Tinn, raising an eyebrow.

"Yeah. I mean, all those years I was trapped by the Dream Stealers, I think I was meant to wait and help you, and maybe you were sent to help me."

"Such things wouldn't surprise me, Noelle. I for one am very glad that we met."

"Mr. Tinn?"

"Yes, Noelle?"

"I want you to know that I believe what you said about the Knights. They ain't just a fairy tale, they're real."

"Ah, so I have made a believer of you?"

"You bet. I'd give anything to be a Knight, and I ain't just sayin' that, honest. You said I only know a little bit of what I can do. So you gotta teach me the rest, right?"

A tremulous smile broke across his face. "You don't give up easily, do you?"

"Nope."

"First of all, we must get out of here," continued Tinn. "Then we'll see about your training."

Noelle grinned. From somewhere behind them came the distant sound of goblins chanting.

"We should try to move faster," she said, taking more of the old man's weight.

Tinn groaned with the effort, and they hurried on, the cries of the goblins growing louder behind them.

38

For what seemed like hours, no one said a word. Zac and the others simply stared at Gideon in disbelief.

Finally, Cornelius broke the silence.

"Gideon, it was you? You were the Dream Stealers' spy?"

Gideon looked at each of them. He looked quite strange now, almost like a different person.

"I am sorry, Cornelius," he said with a shrug. "I had no choice."

"All the way, the Dream Stealers have been one step ahead," said Granny. "Did you tell them everything?"

"Of course," replied Gideon. "I told them that Tinn would be in the Eternal Forest on the night of his capture, and where they could find the second locator compass."

He couldn't quite look at Tom and Tilly.

"But I didn't think they would try to kill your mother," he said weakly.

"How dare you talk to them!" yelled Cornelius, standing in front of his grandchildren. But Granny seemed very calm.

"And what about the werewolf ambush back at Port Town?" she said. "Did you arrange that, too?"

"I'm rather afraid I did, Mrs. Wonder," said Gideon.

"But you saved us!" said Zac. "You saved Granny from that werewolf. I saw you."

"The werewolves had been instructed to keep your grandmother alive," said Gideon. "But they were out of control. I had to intervene. I saved Mrs. Wonder because I still had your trust, and I knew that I could deliver you to the vampires myself. And, sure enough, you followed me here like loyal dogs."

"What about Julius?" said Tom. "You accused *him* of being the spy."

"Julius was beginning to have suspicions," said Gideon. "But he is rather weak. I knew I could shut him up by making him doubt his own mind. The easiest way to do that was to go on the offensive and accuse *him* of being the traitor."

Zac was stunned.

"But why, Gideon?" said Granny.

"Why?" Gideon said, his voice shaking with emotion. "Because the Knights cannot win. You have already lost. How can you ever hope to defeat an enemy that is willing to go to any lengths to claim victory? How can you ever hope to fight fairly against someone who is willing to do things you would never dream of? The Dream Stealers are more powerful now than you can imagine. When they make their move, nothing will stop them. Is it really worth sacrificing your lives because you disagree with their beliefs?"

Cornelius erupted. "Beliefs? Their beliefs are based solely on greed! What they do is wrong, Gideon. Beyond wrong! It is a violation. There is no amount of power to be gained that justifies the torture of dreaming spirits. Yet Dream Stealers are happy to plunder the Dream Plains each night like the filthy bandits they are."

"You don't know how it feels, Cornelius!" said Gideon, a strange, twisted smile creeping over his waxy face. "You can only imagine. When you feed on the fear of a Wakeling, you can actually see the magic flowing into your body! Of course, it is regrettable that the Wakelings suffer, but when you think of what we are gaining, it seems a small price to pay."

"And what price will the Waking World have to pay if the Dream Stealers get their way?" said Granny, her voice low and steady. "What happens when Dream Stealers rule Nocturne, when there is an ever-growing number of people greedy for dark magic? Will you suck the Waking World dry? Will you drive Wakelings mad to satisfy your craving?"

"They will not die," said Gideon.

"And nor will they be truly alive," said Granny. "What they'll suffer will be worse than death. And the people of Nocturne will be no better off. Those who don't join you will be killed, or tortured into insanity. We can't stand by and let that happen."

"Then I'm afraid this is where we part," said Gideon with a shrug. "Good-bye, my dear Knights."

Swinging his pouch full of swag, he turned and walked to the door, nodding at the lead Dream Stealer. Then he glanced once more at the Knights and disappeared into the dark.

"Coward!" yelled Tom.

Twist stepped forward, his lopsided mouth in a contorted smile. "Last chance, Mrs. Wonder. Let's go."

"Oh, I don't think so," she said, deftly unscrewing the arm from her glasses.

Zac was swallowed up by fear. He could see that Granny was ready to fight—but just how strong was the Dream Stealers' dark magic? Then he felt a surge of heat rushing to his fingertips, and the more he thought about the danger facing Granny and his friends, the hotter his fingers became, until at last they felt as if they might burst into flames.

Twist stepped toward Granny. "Take her!" he spat.

Blinding light erupted from Zac's hands, filling the room. There were cries of shock, and the sound of spells being fired, and then the light was gone. Zac dropped to his knees. Everyone was stumbling around, trying to adjust to the darkness. Zac clambered up and walked into a wall. There was another flash of light as Granny stunned one of the Dream Stealers. Someone grabbed Zac's hand and dragged him across the room, and then he was lurching after Cornelius through the darkened passageway and up the stairs.

Granny threw open the front door and they rushed out into the night.

"What happened back there, Zac?" she said.

"I don't know —"

A terrible noise filled the empty darkness. It was a deafening, screeching call.

"It's Raven!" said Tom. "He's calling the other vampires. I read about it in *Myth and* —"

"This way!" Cornelius hollered, leading them up a winding lane. Blood pounded in Zac's ears as he followed. He caught a movement in the corner of his eye and turned to see something that made the blood freeze in his veins.

Vampires were spilling from every door and window. They crawled on the walls like huge shadowy spiders and called out to one another with terrible, shrieking cries.

"They're everywhere!" he shouted. "Come on!"

With shadows closing in, they swung around the corner, and Zac could see what looked like a crumbling church looming over the village. As they ran toward it, it became clear that the stone had been blackened by smoke and fire, and there were places where the building had been ripped apart.

"We're surrounded," said Granny. "I think the church is our best chance. Cornelius?"

"Let's head to the roof," he said. "At least we'll be able to see them coming."

39

Tinn was leaning more and more heavily on Noelle. She was leading the way now, following the dial on the locator compass. Behind them in the dark, they sensed the goblins were closing the gap.

The trees were becoming sparse. Noelle's heart quickened. Perhaps they were approaching the boundary of the Eternal Forest. Sure enough, a little farther on they reached open ground. Noelle stopped in her tracks.

Ahead of them was a cliff face, stretching up at least fifty feet.

"No!" she said. "Not now. We're nearly there, I can feel it!"

She looked at the compass. It was pointing straight at the rock.

"What do we do?" she said, turning to Tinn. His face was ghostly.

"We climb."

"You ain't able!"

"I will manage," he said.

"But what if you can't?"

"Then you will leave me behind," said Tinn. "Do not argue! And when you reach the summit you will run. Do you understand?"

Noelle stared at him, tears in her eyes. She threw her arms around him.

"Ouch!"

"Sorry," she said, unclasping him and wiping her face.

Then Noelle began to climb. It was easier than she had expected, as there were many footholds. In just a few minutes, she was almost a third of the way up the cliff, and she stopped to check on Tinn. He was coming up slowly behind her.

"Keep moving!" he yelled.

Noelle forced herself to continue. It was so hard not to turn back.

On she climbed. The cliff top was almost within reach. Her arms and legs started to ache, and the sharp rock cut into her hands, but she ignored the pain and struggled upward. At last, with one final push, she was lying on the snow-covered grass, gasping for breath. She'd made it.

She clambered to her feet and saw she was on the edge of a small village. It seemed deserted. The houses were falling apart, and some looked as if they had been torched. Narrow lanes and alleyways wound into the darkness.

Breathless and exhausted, Noelle somehow forced her legs to carry her to the village, where she banged on the first door she came to.

"Help! Please help!"

There was no reply. The other houses were in total darkness. She spotted an old barn and rushed toward it. When she reached the doors, she became invisible and passed straight through. Inside, old rusty tools hung from the walls, and several bales of hay had been stacked in a pile. Then she saw it: a length of rope dangling from a beam. She grabbed it and headed back to the cliff.

There were a few trees near the cliff edge. She selected the sturdiest and tied one end of the rope around its trunk, then began lowering the other end toward Tinn. He still had a way to climb.

Beneath, there was a terrible chanting, and Noelle's heart skipped a beat as goblins began bounding from the forest and onto the cliff.

"Mr. Tinn!" she yelled. "Grab hold of the rope!"

She peered over the edge. The rope was swinging precariously beside Rumpous Tinn, who was doing his very best to grasp it. The goblins had started firing arrows again, and Noelle had to dodge more than one as she kept the line steady.

She felt a sharp tug as Tinn managed to clutch the rope.

"Keep climbing!" she yelled. "I'll take some of the weight!"

She heaved with all of her might. It was working! He was climbing much more quickly than before, and soon he was almost at the summit.

"I told you to run!" he yelled through gritted teeth.

"Be quiet and climb!" shouted Noelle, and soon Tinn was lying in a heap in the snow beside her.

The old man was so pale he looked almost transparent, and weak little puffs of steam hung in the freezing air as he struggled to breathe. Noelle was scared.

"Come on," she said. "We have to get you indoors."

Tinn did not answer. He merely leaned on her and allowed himself to be led away. As they went, Noelle could hear ominous scraping noises from the cliff. The goblins would soon reach the top, too.

She and Tinn cut along one of the narrow alleyways, which took them past row after row of spooky, crumbling houses.

"I've a bad feeling about this place, Mr. Tinn," she whispered. "Something's not right."

They turned out of the lane and into a deserted square, where the skeleton of a church stood high over the village.

"Come on," panted Noelle. "We can hide in there."

She led Tinn toward the church, and pushed the battered door gently. It creaked open and they slipped inside.

The building was a shell. The smell of fire still lingered, and the stained-glass windows were blackened and shattered. Most of the benches were burned to ash, and flecks of snow fell through large holes in the roof.

Noelle helped Tinn past the scorched wood and crumbling stone to a seat on a fallen statue. When she was sure the old man was comfortable, she set to bolting the doors. They were misshapen, and it wasn't easy, but eventually she managed to close them and return to his side.

"Mr. Tinn?" she said softly.

He gazed at her through glassy eyes and coughed.

"I would like to thank you, Noelle," he said, his voice weak. "You have shown courage, kindness, and bravery — far more than that of an average person. I have been thinking about what you asked of me, and I have come to my decision. If I make it out of this with my life, I shall take it upon myself to make you a Knight's apprentice. Perhaps you were correct after all. Perhaps we were supposed to meet. I am beginning to suspect, Noelle, that you may have a part to play in Nocturne's future."

Noelle grinned widely. "Oh, thank you, Mr. Tinn! You ain't gonna regret this, I promise—"

A terrible noise enveloped them—a deafening, grating screech—and they instinctively covered their ears.

"What in Nod was that?" said Tinn, wide-eyed. "Noelle, what's wrong?"

Noelle could hardly move. She knelt beside Tinn, shaking violently. It couldn't be. Not again.

"I've heard that noise," she whispered, "one time before, when I was only little. It's the sound I heard the night our village was attacked. It's the call of a vampire, the call of their leader."

"Are you sure?"

"I'll not forget it, not ever."

"Then we must leave," said Tinn, struggling to his knees. "But first, I wonder if you couldn't do me one last favor?"

"Just name it."

"I was wondering, Noelle, if you'd be so kind as to pull this arrow from my back?"

"What? Me? I don't know anythin' about treatin' wounds. What if I pull it out wrong? What if I pull it out and there's a lung on the end of it?"

"I will take that chance," said Tinn with a little smile. "I have been able to hold off the goblin's arrow poison thus far, but it is beginning to take its toll."

Noelle wrapped her shaking hands around the shaft of the arrow. She felt queasy.

"You ready?" she asked.

Tinn closed his eyes and nodded.

"OK," she said slowly. "Here goes. One . . . two . . . THREE!"

She pulled hard and felt the arrowhead rip from Tinn's back. The old man let out a howl of agony and slumped to the floor. There were patches of deep red all over his white robes.

"Mr. Tinn," she said, "you all right?"

"I have been better," he grimaced. "But that had to be done. Goblin arrows, you see, have a rather nasty habit of carrying some potent poisons. In this instance I think I have been lucky. If this arrow had contained one of the more deadly strains, I might already be, well, dead!"

He took a deep breath and, groaning loudly, managed to get to his feet without her help. "I shall have to buy new clothes," he said with the hint of a smile.

BANG!

Noelle whirled around. "What was that?"

THUMP!

Tinn stared past her. "Come, we must hide," he said.

They sneaked back among the shadows, holding their breath.

BANG!

The door was blasted open. Noelle peered out, expecting to see a swarm of stinking goblins pouring into the church. Instead a motley group of people stood in the doorway. There were three children, an old man in a long black coat and cowboy hat, and a stout old lady who seemed to be clutching her spectacles tightly in her hand.

40

"Good work, Cornelius!" said Granny.

Cornelius tipped his hat and forged ahead through the gloomy church.

"This way," he said. "Up to the roof."

Zac and the others followed him through a small doorway to a steep staircase. They bounded up the steps and through a rickety door on to a wide, flat roof. Snow had begun to fall and the wind had picked up. Cornelius ran to the edge and peered over the low wall.

"They're coming!" he yelled.

Shrieking calls signaled the vampire takeoff. Dark shadows filled the air.

All around him, Zac could see hovering vampires

attempting to land on the roof while the Knights fought desperately to keep them at bay, lighting the darkness with flashes of blazing magic.

"Look out!"

Someone pushed him to the floor as a wayward spell streaked overhead.

"What the—?"

The air fluttered and a fearsome-looking girl appeared from nowhere. She stuck out her hand.

Puzzled, Zac did the only thing he could think of and grasped it. A powerful electric feeling shot up his arm.

"Owww!" they cried in unison.

"What was that?" cried Zac, staring at his hand.

"I haven't a clue, but we haven't time for that now. I'm Noelle," said the girl. "I'm here with Rumpous Tinn."

"Tinn is *here*?" exclaimed Zac. "We've been searching for him!"

"He's on his way," she said.

Zac glanced across the rooftop. Cornelius was struggling with one vampire, Granny was desperately fighting another two, and Tom and Tilly were dodging attacks from every direction.

"I wish he'd hurry up!" he said.

Among the shadows in the burnt-out church below, Rumpous Tinn hobbled toward the staircase.

High above, he could hear yells and screams and exploding spells. Through a hole in the roof, he saw flashes of colored light. He knew his friends were up there, and by the sound of it they were in trouble. Injured as he was, he was still their best chance.

When he reached the doorway, something made him stop in his tracks. The air inside the church had suddenly changed. It seemed to be crackling with magic.

And then he heard a voice, metallic and grating.

"Mr. Tinn. What a pleasant surprise this is."

Tinn turned slowly. Shadow stood in the aisle, a dark ghost, her long black cloak trailing on the ash-covered floor.

"It's over," she said. "You are weak. Your friends are outnumbered and outmatched. Accept defeat."

"I may be injured," said Tinn with a grimace, "but I can assure you that there is still fight in this old body." He straightened up.

For what seemed an age nothing happened. Sounds from the battle above echoed through the cavernous space. Tinn and Shadow stood perfectly still, staring, each waiting for the other to strike first.

At last Shadow moved. She spun majestically, her arms outstretched. The air around her seemed to glow for a moment. And then a blinding shockwave thundered through the church. Tinn had no time to react. He was thrown back against the wall and dumped heavily on the floor.

Then he stood up. The adrenaline of battle seemed to have freed him from the pain of his injury. He smiled.

"My turn," he said.

"HA!" Granny let out a yell of triumph as her spell hit a particularly horrid vampire. But her jubilation was short-lived; more of them were arriving every minute — among them, Raven. The leader of the vampires bared his fangs as he advanced toward them.

Zac found a wooden plank buried in the snow and began swinging it wildly at any monster that came too near. As Granny ran to him, Zac noticed she looked exhausted. The Knights were tiring with every spell they fired. A bolt of fear struck him.

They couldn't hang on forever.

BOOM!

The whole building shook. A beam of white light erupted from the hole in the roof, reaching into the sky like a searchlight. A moment later it was gone.

"What in Nocturne was that?" said Granny.

Thwack! Thwack! Thwack!

Raven stopped in his tracks as three arrows plunged into his body. He threw back his head and screamed in pain and anger. Suddenly there were dark shapes pouring over the church wall, attacking anything that moved.

"Goblins!" yelled Granny.

BOOM!

The door to the staircase was blown clear across the roof. Two figures came stomping out into the open, dueling wildly. The first was an old man with blood-soaked white robes and a bushy white beard; the second was a woman in a sparkling black skull mask and long black coat.

Zac felt the air become heavy with magic.

Rumpous Tinn had arrived, but so had the Dream Stealers.

41

"It's Tinn!" yelled Granny. "He's here!"

Tinn and Shadow were lighting up the entire village with explosions of awesome magic. The searing heat from their spells was almost overpowering. Zac had never experienced anything like it. His hair was standing on end.

Shadow began to force Tinn to his knees. Seeing their friend in trouble, Cornelius and Granny tried to make their way toward him, but before either of them could get close, Shadow spun around and sent both of them careering across the roof with a powerful blast of dark magic.

Suddenly, the air beside Zac fluttered and Noelle

appeared next to him. Zac felt the strange electricity course through his veins again.

"We have to do something," Noelle said.

"Like what?" said Zac. "How can we possibly fight her? Look at what she's done to everyone else!"

"Try to distract her," snapped Noelle. "I'll think of something." And she disappeared again.

"Distract her. Great idea!"

WHAM!

Zac hit the floor. Then another blow hit him hard in the face. He gazed up blearily to see the lopsided Dream Stealer sneering down at him.

"Gotcha," Twist snarled, unsheathing a small sword.

Zac closed his eyes. This was it. He was going to die, and he hadn't even been able to help Noelle.

WHACK! A fist came from nowhere and smacked Twist across his ugly face. As the Dream Stealer folded to the ground, Zac looked up again to see a tall handsome boy standing over him, his dark wavy hair falling across his forehead.

Zac froze as the boy took his arm and pulled him to his feet. To his shock, as the boy's hand wrapped around his arm, Zac felt the same surge of electricity as when he had touched Noelle's hand. The boy snarled and stepped back, revealing a sharp set of fangs.

A vampire!

"Who are you?" spluttered Zac.

The boy shook his head. "I can't explain . . ." He turned Zac to face Shadow and Tinn. "Go! Help!"

When Zac glanced back, the boy had disappeared.

A friendly vampire? Surely there was no such thing . . . But there was no time to ponder his strange encounter; Noelle and Tinn needed him.

In a confused daze, Zac began to stumble toward Shadow. How on earth was he going to distract her? She'd squish him like a pesky bug.

But, as he grew nearer, he felt a great heat building in his fingers again. This time he knew what it was. Magic.

Tinn was still on his knees. Shadow stood before him, her dagger drawn.

Zac let the magic erupt from his fingertips. A jet of scorching light tore through the night and hit Shadow in the back. She screamed and dropped her dagger onto the roof, then spun to face Zac.

He had her attention.

"Great," he muttered. "Now what?"

Shaking uncontrollably, Zac stood his ground as Shadow began to walk determinedly toward him. He flexed his hands desperately, hoping for more magic, but nothing happened. Shadow was only a few paces away, and nobody—not Granny or Cornelius, or even Rumpous Tinn—could help.

Then, just as Shadow reached out to throw her deadly spell, the air fluttered behind her. Noelle appeared, fury etched on her face. She had retrieved Shadow's dagger and was clutching it purposefully. With a yell, Noelle leapt in the air and brought the dagger down as hard as she could, driving it deep into the Dream Stealer leader's back.

Shadow's scream was terrible. Zac turned away, covering his aching ears. As he did so he saw Tinn scrabble to his feet. In the next instant, the old man charged at Shadow, pushing her toward the edge of the roof, and the Dream Stealer leader toppled, spinning through the snow to the ground far below.

At that moment, the whole sky seemed to light up.

Zac was half blinded. The light appeared to be dancing on the roof. He heard the sound of a sputtering engine.

High above them, a rusty old camper van was being flung around in the wind. Its dazzling spotlight wavered among the snowflakes as it searched the church roof. Zac had never been so pleased to see anything in his entire life.

"Granny!" he yelled. "Look! It's *Nightstalker*. Mr. Sundown has come to help!"

Granny, back on her feet, paused for a moment to look up. A smile flashed across her wrinkled face. Then she noticed Twist trying to pick himself up nearby, and she kicked him hard in the backside. With a pathetic scream, he tumbled over the edge of the roof.

"Get ready to move!" she shouted over the rabble.

Nightstalker was bobbing high above the battleground like a boat in stormy waters. The door fell open and the outline of a figure appeared. A rope ladder unfurled in the air, and the figure leapt from the hatch and slid down toward the roof. When he landed, the ship's spotlight passed over him, and Zac saw his face clearly. It was Julius!

As Julius joined the fray, Tinn yelled instructions and began to scatter goblins and vampires alike.

"Make for the ladder! The children first!"

Energized by Shadow's defeat, the Knights fought with renewed strength toward the foot of the ladder, where they formed a tight circle.

"Tom, you first," said Zac, seeing his friend's battered face. Tilly was next, followed by Noelle. Then it was Zac's turn. He clutched the ladder tightly and began to climb. Above him, Tom and Tilly were already safely in the cabin. Noelle was almost there, too. The ladder jerked as Granny, Cornelius, and Julius climbed on below. Finally, Rumpous Tinn fired a parting spell and leapt from the ledge of the roof, grabbing the ladder. Granny gave a yell of elation. They were off!

Thwack!

Agonizing, red-hot pain erupted in Zac's leg, spreading quickly up his body. His blood felt as if it had turned to acid. Terrified, he looked down. A large arrow was buried deeply in his thigh. Then the world began to swirl, and he was falling.

A hand caught his wrist, and Zac swung helplessly in the air. The cold wind and snow battered him as the *Nightstalker* gathered speed. And then he was being carried up the ladder to feel the warmth of the ship's cabin wrap around him like a blanket. He lay shivering on the floor, and his eyes met Granny's. She smiled, a tear rolling down her cheek.

"It's all right, lad," she said. "It's going to be all right."

As Rigby Sundown swung the ship out into the night sky, Zac felt someone tugging at the arrow in his leg. There was a moment of shattering pain and he felt the last of his energy leave him.

He closed his eyes. A veil of color draped itself around the world, and he drifted off toward the shimmering light of the Dream Plains as *Nightstalker* cut through the snowflakes, blazing a path to safety.

42

Light and color shifted in a glittering infinity of patterns.

As he flew through the Dream Plains, Zac felt a great rush of freedom. He knew he'd seen this wondrous place before, but never like this.

His mind was foggy. How did he get here? And how long had it been since he arrived? Hours? Days? Time seemed not to matter anymore.

Eventually, the blurred tangle of thoughts in his mind began to clear. He realized the pain in his leg had gone. He looked down and saw the most remarkable thing. Where the solid form of his body would usually have been, there was only a wispy ribbon of smoke. As he concentrated, the smoke curled and twisted, slowly creating the outline of the body he had expected to see. He raised a hand and the smoke rolled and billowed, forming fingers in front of his eyes.

How strange.

Now he could hear voices whispering in the distance. He floated toward them.

And then he felt it.

Fear.

He knew somehow that the fear wasn't his own. It belonged to someone else, but it was terrible just the same, and he needed to find it, to stop it.

He flew down through the mist until he reached what he thought must be the ground, and there he saw another figure, made of glowing smoke just as he was. This figure was an old man, and he was running from something. He kept glancing over his shoulder at his pursuer, moans and wails spilling from his mouth as he stumbled away.

Zac opened his mouth and discovered that he had a voice.

"Hey, wait," he called.

And now he saw what was in pursuit.

A skull, swooping through the mist.

As it drew nearer, Zac realized it wasn't a floating skull at all. It was a man. The figure was wearing a shining silver mask, and his silver-armored arms were crossed over his chest. He wasn't made of smoke. He was flesh and bone.

A Dream Stealer.

The old man stopped and faced the creature, dropping to his knees.

"Please!" he wailed. "Please, no."

The Dream Stealer laughed coldheartedly, and sent a ball of black smoke hurtling through the mist toward him. The ball engulfed the old man completely for a second. Then the dark magic fell back and began to shift and change. It took the form of an old woman, lying on the ground, wailing in agony and reaching out to grab him.

Zac understood what he was seeing. The old man was being made to experience his worst fear. This was how the Dream Stealers hunted.

He moved forward, placing himself between the Dream Stealer and his victim. All at once, the haunting old lady vanished, and the cloud of black smoke gathered around Zac, but he felt no fear or pain or anger. Zac looked the Dream Stealer in the face and saw the bony arms tremble.

With a rush of power, Zac blew the dark magic back toward the Dream Stealer. It swirled about him like a tornado, faster and faster, until at last it exploded in a blinding flash. The Dream Stealer was hurled into the mist and the old man's smoky outline floated freely away like a raindrop into a river.

Smiling, Zac pushed back more dark clouds and bolts of dark magic, letting the beautiful dreams flood back onto the Dream Plains: here a dream of swimming in blue seas; there of flying in winged chariots; and there of singing choirs. They swept over the Dream Plains like waves of happiness. His power was stronger than he could ever have imagined! The Dream Stealers were finally on the run.

Zac knew there were more dreaming Wakelings out there, Wakelings he could help. Now he realized exactly what he was destined to do.

And it was going to be fun.

43

Eventually, the Dream Plains faded. The whispers fell silent.

Zac Wonder stirred from a deep sleep to the unmistakeable smell of fresh cinnamon creeping up his nostrils.

"Hello, Zac."

He sat up with a start. He was lying on a four-poster bed in a comfortable room with large windows and a fluffy purple carpet. Granny was sitting in a deep armchair by the foot of his bed.

"Granny! Where am I? Is everyone OK?"

She raised her hand to quiet him, the corners of her mouth twitching.

"Everyone's fine, lad," she said.

"How long have I been asleep?"

"Just over a week."

"What? How long?"

"Goblin poison is powerful stuff, Zac," she said. "I was very scared we might lose you."

"Am I in the hospital? Sweet Dreams?" He looked out the window and saw the shadow of Slumber Mountain.

"That's right. How's your leg?"

Zac hadn't thought about it. He felt his thigh, where the arrow had plunged deep under his skin. It was bandaged heavily.

"It burns a little, but it's not that bad."

"Good."

Granny sat back in the armchair and reached for her pipe, only to realize that she couldn't smoke it in the hospital. She packed it away again and sighed.

"I'm very proud of you, lad," she said.

Zac smiled. "Everyone else is really all right?"

"I told you, they're all fine," she said with a chuckle. "Tinn was injured, but he'll be OK. It's a good thing Julius went back to fetch Mr. Sundown. If they hadn't arrived when they did, we'd have all been in real trouble."

"So that's where Julius went back in Port Town?" said Zac. "He went to fetch Sundown?"

"Julius was certain Gideon was working for the Dream Stealers," said Granny. "But he didn't have any proof. Nor did he want to jeopardize the mission. The morning we reached Port Town, he sneaked away to find Sundown. He asked him to join us — his thinking was that if we had Sundown's ship, we'd be able to escape any trap Gideon had set for us. Sundown was ready for another adventure, of course, but by the time they got back to the inn we'd already been attacked, and Gideon had led us away. Julius and Sundown asked around, and heard we were headed in the direction of that terrible vampire village. They followed — and thank the stars they did."

"I still can't believe Gideon was working for the Dream Stealers," said Zac. "How could he lead his friends into a trap like that?"

"Gideon was seduced by dark magic," Granny said sadly. "It has happened before and it'll happen again." She leaned forward in the armchair, her little eyes serious. "There is potential for darkness in all of us, lad — and there comes a time when we must choose which path to follow. For someone who is tired and frightened, for someone who has lost all hope, dark magic, with all its hollow promises, is the easy choice. And that's the difference — *hope*. As long as you have that hope, as long as you have something to fight *for*, darkness will never extinguish the light in your spirit completely. Gideon lost his hope. He made his choice."

There was a knock on the door. Rumpous Tinn poked his head into the room.

"Mind if I crash the party?" he said.

"Come on in, Rumpous," said Granny.

Tinn closed the door behind him and hobbled over to the bed. He was leaning heavily on a wooden cane with a golden handle carved into the shape of a crescent moon.

"May I sit down?" he asked.

"Of course."

Tinn clicked his fingers and an empty armchair left its place under the window. It sped across the carpet and stopped right behind him.

"Well now, Zac," he began, plopping himself down on the chair, "I've heard so much about you from Tom and Tilly it's hard to believe we've never been introduced. I am Rumpous Tinn, and it is a great pleasure to finally meet you."

"Thanks," said Zac. "You, too."

"Would you like a toffee?" Tinn asked. "I bought them from old Saccharina Fudge's shop this morning. They're the best, you know."

"Yes, please," said Zac, and much to his surprise, Tinn reached into his white beard and began to rummage around.

"Let's see . . . I know they're in here somewhere . . . ah!"

He produced a little brown paper bag, opened it, and

clicked his fingers. Three chunks of toffee shot up into the air and floated there, spinning like miniature asteroids. Tinn casually waved his hand and two of the pieces flew gently across the room, into the open hands of Zac and Granny. The other piece sailed into Tinn's mouth.

After a few minutes of loud chewing, Tinn looked from Granny to Zac, his lined face becoming very serious.

"I want to thank you both for everything," he said. "If it hadn't been for you, the Knights of Nod might be nothing more than a memory. I would also like permission, Eve, to explain to Zac why all of this is happening. I feel he deserves that much."

"Very well," said Granny, examining her fingernails.

Zac sat forward in bed. He had the feeling things were about to get interesting.

"Fifty years ago," began Tinn, "I had just taken up the post of Grandmaster. We were on the verge of victory against the Dream Stealers when, one evening, an oracle burst into our camp."

"What's an oracle?" asked Zac.

"Someone who can see glimpses of the future," said Granny.

"This oracle had seen a terrible future," Tinn continued. "He told me the Dream Stealers would return in half a century under a leader of immeasurable strength, and bring about a time of great suffering—a time known as the Darkness. The oracle said there were only three people who could stop the Dream Stealers—a Trinity of heroes who could save us all. Unfortunately, his vision ended before he was able to reveal to us the identity of all those heroes. The only name he could give us was your grandmother's."

"Granny?" sputtered Zac.

"In those days, spies were everywhere," said Tinn. "Word of the oracle soon reached the Dream Stealers. Luckily, they never learned that your granny was one of the Trinity. I hid her in the Waking World, where I knew she'd be safe. When the Dream Stealers showed up again recently—half a century later as predicted—I knew it was time for her to return. Unfortunately, they seem to have put the pieces of the puzzle together and realized that we were protecting her for a very good reason."

"And that's why the Dream Stealers want her?" said Zac. "They know she's important? But that means she'll never be safe."

"None of us will ever be safe while the Dream Stealers are around, Zac," said Granny.

"But what if the oracle was wrong?" Zac pressed.

"I'm afraid there's no chance of that," Tinn said sadly. "Everything he predicted has so far come true. I hope you can understand why you were dragged into all of this. You almost lost your life. For that I am truly sorry."

"I'm not sorry, sir," said Zac. "I love it here. I've never felt like I belong in the Waking World. Part of me's always wanted to run away. I think I've found where it wanted to run to."

Granny and Tinn shared a smile.

"He *is* a natural," she said.

"Ah, yes," said Tinn. "I gather you have been astounding the Knights with your own talents, Zac?"

"Me?" he gasped.

"I have heard all about the dreams you have been experiencing. I know about the dream orb, the werewolf, the dagger—which, incidentally, Tilly has handed over and I shall be examining carefully. Dream orbs can be dangerous things, and I'm afraid my sister had an unhealthy obsession with them. You did well to survive. Your grandmother has also informed me that you warned the Knights of a werewolf attack in Port Town, quite possibly saving their lives. I assume you also saw this in your sleep?"

"Yes, sir."

"And strange things have happened to you in times of danger, yes? You have performed magic?"

"Back on the church roof!" Zac spluttered. "The invisible girl . . . Noelle . . . asked me to distract that terrible woman with the mask and . . . and the magic just sort of happened. But I don't know how I did it—any of it."

"You did it just the same," said Tinn. "It seems clear to me that you are in possession of certain gifts, Zac, gifts that could prove most useful indeed. That is why I'd like you to become a Knight's apprentice. I believe your granny would be more than happy to teach you."

Zac's eyes almost jumped out of their sockets. "Really?" he said.

The old man chuckled. "The final decision lies with your grandmother," he said, shooting a look at Granny. "What do you say, Eve?"

Granny sat back in her chair and polished her glasses. She took a long, hard look at Zac. "Couldn't do any harm, I suppose," she said. The faintest smile crossed her lips.

"Then it is decided," said Tinn.

Zac felt like leaping out of his bed and running around the room. He was going to learn magic. Real magic! And then something else struck him. A flash of light and color crossed his mind, and a memory came flooding back. "Mr. Tinn, there's something else . . ."

"Of course there is," said Tinn with a smile. "And what exactly might it be, Zac?"

"Well, while I was sleeping all that time . . . I had the strangest dream. It was like . . . like I was in the Dream Plains. I could see Wakelings' dreams, and I could stop the Dream Stealers from turning them into nightmares. They couldn't attack me—I could deflect their dark magic and chase them off. The dream keeps repeating, over and over again, but slightly different each time."

A look of great surprise crossed Tinn's face, and the old man met Granny's gaze for a long moment before answering calmly.

"Zac," he began, "do you know that while you have been asleep, the Dream Stealers have ceased attacking Wakeling spirits in the Dream Plains?"

Zac's mouth fell open. "You think *I* had something to do with that? You think I wasn't just dreaming?"

"I cannot be sure," said Tinn. He thought carefully for a few seconds, as though making up his mind. "Zac, when the oracle told me your grandmother was one of the Trinity . . . well . . . that wasn't quite the whole story. He never actually gave us her full name. He only ever said 'Wonder.'"

"Now hang on a minute, Rumpous," said Granny sharply.

"All I'm saying is, there's more than one person in this room who answers to that name," said Tinn, holding up his hands.

Zac let this wash over him for a moment. "So you're saying the oracle might have been talking about me and not Granny?"

"Rubbish!" yelled Granny. "He's a child!"

"And where is it written that children are not capable

of great and daring acts?" said Tinn. He looked at Zac, his eyes twinkling. "Your experience in the Dream Plains, Zac, the dream you mentioned — and the fact that you can dream at all in Nocturne — makes me think that it is very possible the name Wonder referred to you. Furthermore, Noelle has described something rather strange to me. She said that when you first met her on the church roof, something happened — a magical energy passed between you. Is this correct?"

"Yes, sir. It was like . . . like electricity. Do you think it means something?"

Tinn rubbed his head. "Yes, Zac, I do. I think it may mean we have found another member of the Trinity."

"You mean Noelle?"

"Indeed. There are cases throughout history, although admittedly very few, where a small group of people have been closely connected by magic. I have never seen this for myself until now, but I have read several theories on the phenomenon. It seems that, when brought together, the magical power of these people is increased. While we were escaping from the Dream Stealer lair, Noelle continued to surprise me with her talent. I have a feeling she might be special, and I have told her as much. I believe you share such a connection with her."

"Enough!" said Granny. "I won't let you put Zac's life in danger like this. If the Dream Stealers find out that you believe he's one of the Trinity—"

"But that's just the point, Eve," said Tinn. "They haven't the foggiest! In fact, they believe *you* are the threat. If we keep it that way, then we may be able to protect Zac—to take the heat off him, as it were."

This seemed to get Granny thinking, and Zac took the opportunity to ask another question.

"Back at the church," he began, "something else happened. Just before I hit Shadow with that spell, that ugly Dream Stealer attacked me. I thought I was a goner. And then . . . then this vampire helped me! A boy."

"Are you certain he was a vampire?" said Granny.

"I'm sure. I saw his fangs. But I haven't got to the *really* strange part yet."

"What do you mean?"

"Well, he helped me up, and when he touched me, I felt the same magical electricity as I did with Noelle. If that energy means we're connected—that *we're* the Trinity—then something's up, because that would mean one of the Trinity is a vampire."

Tinn looked thoughtful, as though deciding on something with great care. "It is entirely possible," he said at last. "I wonder how I could have overlooked . . ."

"But who is he?" pressed Zac. "How do we find him? And how can we convince him to help us?"

"Let's not worry about that for the moment," said

Tinn. "What you have revealed to me is interesting—very interesting indeed. I shall think on the matter. In the meantime, if I am correct, we have definitely found two of the Trinity, two missing pieces of the jigsaw. Is something the matter, Eve?"

Granny was looking glum. "If Zac really is one of the Trinity," she said, "then I suppose there's nothing I can do about it. But I want your promise, Rumpous, that he'll be kept as safe as possible."

"Granny," said Zac, "I don't need to be packed in bubble wrap."

"You have my word, Eve," said Tinn solemnly.

Zac's head was spinning. "So what now?" he said.

Tinn stood up with a groan and leaned heavily on his cane. "Now? We enjoy Christmas! After that? Well, I have a few ideas, but we'll get to those soon enough. And I would certainly recommend that you develop your mysterious ability to fend off Dream Stealers."

Zac nodded.

"Oh, Mr. Tinn?"

"Yes, dear boy?"

"I was just wondering. If the Dream Stealers manage to repair the other locator compass . . . will they be able to use it to find the Knights?" The thought of Dream Stealers creeping into The Forty Winks and murdering his friends made Zac's blood turn to ice.

"They'll have quite a job. They'll have to break the binding spell I cast over it first," said Tinn kindly. "And you'll be glad to know that because of Gideon's treachery, the protective enchantments surrounding The Forty Winks have been reset and are now powerful enough to withstand even the strongest magic. Of that I am sure." He tapped the side of his nose.

Zac felt a rush of relief.

"Now," said Tinn, "I do hate to dash off, but there are things to be done. The life of a Grandmaster is rather a busy one. I've had a word with the people downstairs. They'll let you go home tomorrow."

"Christmas Eve," whispered Granny.

"Thanks, Mr. Tinn," said Zac. The thought of spending Christmas with his new friends made his heart leap.

"Not a problem," said Tinn. He pulled a golden watch from his pocket. "Oh, by the stars!" he said. "I really must be going."

With a cheery wave and a swish of his white robe, the old man swept from the room. After he had gone, Zac and Granny sat in silence for a time.

Questions filled Zac's head to bursting. Why had the Dream Stealers stopped attacking Wakelings so suddenly? Had it really been something to do with his experience in the Dream Plains? Had they stopped for good? Was Granny's job done? Was the Waking World safe? And what about this business with the Trinity? Could Tinn be right? Could he really be one of only three people who could stop the Dream Stealers?

Anyway, he was going to be a Knight. At least, he was going to try. But what if he found out Tinn was wrong? What if he wasn't very good at magic? What if everything he'd done so far had been blind luck? He imagined Rumpous Tinn having to tell Granny that there had been some mistake, and that Zac should just go back to the Waking World. He saw himself pleading to stay, working behind the bar in The Forty Winks and taking orders from Barnaby while Tom and Tilly went off on grand adventures without him.

A little bell rang, signaling the end of visiting hours, and Zac was jerked from his thoughts. Granny wrapped herself up warmly and kissed him on the forehead. He watched her leave, then rolled over to look out the window, thinking of Christmas at The Forty Winks with all his friends.

44

Twist, the lopsided Dream Stealer, lay shivering in bed, his sheets soaked with sweat, even though it was freezing in the tiny cabin. Outside, the wind whistled through the trees, drowning out the snap and crackle of the dying fire.

The slightest creak made him jump.

As soon as he'd lost the Knights back on that church roof, he'd known that he couldn't go back to face Shadow. He'd seen her stabbed by some urchin girl, then thrown from the roof by that ridiculous old man — but he knew deep down that her dark magic would have saved her, and that she would be hungry for revenge. Despite his injuries — including that crushing blow to the head from a *vampire* — he'd managed to make his way to the Eternal Forest. After a day or two of aimless wandering, he'd stumbled upon this cabin, and the kindly old couple who'd lived here had taken him in and treated his wounds. He'd told them he'd been hurt in a hunting accident.

As the days had passed, his strength had begun to grow. He realized he could never return. Shadow would kill him as soon as she set eyes on him. So he'd decided to stay where he was. Getting rid of the old couple had been easy. They were frail, and didn't put up much of a fight. Now he was alone. Shadow would never know. Maybe she'd think he'd been killed in the battle, or taken away and eaten by goblins.

She wouldn't find him here.

She couldn't.

And yet he found himself unable to shake her image from his mind.

At times he thought he could feel her eyes on him . . . sense her searching . . . grasping at the air around him.

He shook himself.

No . . . he was safe here. Nobody even knew he was still breathing.

He closed his eyes. After a while, the gentle patter of snow on the windowpane lulled him into an uneasy sleep.

He was woken in the middle of the night by a tapping on the window.

This time it wasn't the snow.

Dread filled his insides. He pulled the covers over his misshapen face and prayed that whatever it was would just go away.

Tap tap tap.

Twist peeked over the blanket toward the window. The curtains were drawn, but he could see movement outside. Something was there!

He crept from the bed and stood at the window for a moment.

Tap tap tap.

His guts twisted with fear. Slowly, he reached for the curtains, his heart punching against the inside of his chest, and pulled them apart.

He screamed.

Raven, the vampire leader, stared back at him from the other side of the glass.

The Dream Stealer stumbled backward and fell hard onto the cold floor. Blinded by panic, he pulled himself up and headed for the door, tearing it open.

He froze.

Two circles of black glass stared back at him through the falling snow.

"Hello, Twist," said Shadow. "We've been worried about you."

"M-my lady," said Twist, thinking fast. "Thank the stars you have found me! I was injured, and became lost in these woods."

Shadow continued to stare. Raven appeared by her side.

"Aren't you going to invite us in?" he said, flashing his fangs.

"Of course . . . please . . . ," said Twist, stepping aside. Shadow and Raven entered. Twist closed the door and led them over to the warmth of the fire. He noticed Shadow was limping, but otherwise appeared unharmed.

"Sit down," said Shadow.

Without a word, Twist pulled up a simple wooden chair and sat.

She stood over him. "I am disappointed," she said.

"I can explain!" pleaded Twist. "I was hurt!"

"So were others," said Shadow. "And yet they did not scurry away into the darkness like rats. They died fighting. They died in an attempt to stop the Knights of Nod. You were in charge, Twist. You were supposed to deliver Eve Wonder to me. You let her slip through your fingers, and now everything I have worked toward is in danger of falling apart. The Knights are regrouping, growing stronger. If you had done your job, they would not be a problem."

"I can make it up to you," said Twist. "I can help. I'll get to the Dream Plains and feed, I can get my strength back and—"

"That is not possible. I have been forced to ban any of us from entering the Dream Plains."

Twist stared at Shadow in disbelief. "Why?"

"Because something is happening in there," said Shadow. "A new power is present. Dream Stealers are being stalked, hunted."

"By what?"

"I have not seen it for myself," said Shadow. "But those who have call it the Silver Storm. They say it is made from smoke, like the spirit of a Wakeling, but it is immune to our dark magic. It has been protecting Wakelings, turning our spells against us. Since you abandoned us a week ago, a growing number of Dream Stealers have been affected each night. Many say they will never set foot in the Dream Plains again. I cannot allow any more of our number to come into contact with this being until I know more about it."

"Do you think it's something to do with the Knights?"

"I do not know." Shadow looked at Raven.

Raven handed something to the Dream Stealer leader. Twist recognized it instantly — it was his skull mask. Shadow held it up, running her gloved fingers over its surface, and a moment later the mask began to change. Twist watched as it turned to molten metal in Shadow's hand and started to form another shape. Within seconds, Shadow was clutching a gleaming blade.

Twist clasped his hands to his chest. "Please!" he begged. "I can make it up to you. I was going to come back, I was!" He nodded desperately at Raven. "Why have you forgiven *him* so readily?" he demanded. "He lost the Knights, too! He's just as responsible."

Shadow leaned over him, her jet-encrusted mask so close that he could see his own terrified reflection in the circles of black glass over her eyes.

"I have forgiven *him*, Twist, because I still regard him as being of some use. He was able to sniff out your hiding place, for example. You, on the other hand, have outlived your usefulness — and I cannot risk the chance that you might seek out the Knights and offer information in exchange for protection."

"But I'd never —"

The blade flashed in the firelight, and Twist slumped lifelessly to the floor. Shadow tossed the dagger into the fire, where it turned back into a Dream Stealer mask and began to melt.

"There is no time to waste," she said, heading for the door. "Tonight we have rid ourselves of a tiresome insect, but there are others to worry about. We must find a way of exterminating the Knights of Nod. While they survive, my plans are in danger."

"What would you have me do?" said Raven.

"Go back to your village. It would be safer to lay low for now."

"And you, my lady?" said Raven.

Shadow reached into her cloak and produced the unfinished locator compass. It seemed to transfix her for a moment. Raven watched her with interest. She seemed different. Distracted. Worried, even.

"I have much to do," she said finally. She put the instrument back in her cloak and opened the front door to the driving snow. She motioned toward Twist's body. "Enjoy your supper," she said. "I will be in touch."

And then she was gone.

45

"Wake up, mate! It's Christmas!"

Zac leapt out of bed.

"Ouch!"

He'd forgotten about his leg.

"You ought to be careful," said Tom. "You'll end up back in Sweet Dreams. C'mon, let's go!"

Tom raced out into the hallway. Zac hobbled after him as fast as he could.

"Wow!" he heard Tom yell.

Zac sped up. There was an enormous Christmas tree in the hall, just outside the double doors to Tinn's quarters. Below the tree was a mountain of parcels. By the time Zac had caught up with him, Tom had already unwrapped three of his presents. He was holding a golden ticket for a year's subscription to *Myth and Magic*, and had managed to stuff a whole bag of Saccharina Fudge's Finest Treacle Toffee into his mouth.

"Ook at all da pwesents," he managed to say.

Tilly and Noelle appeared and rushed over to the pile of gifts.

"Merry Christmas, everyone," said Tilly.

"Merry Christmas," they replied.

The children ripped into the pile of presents and stuffed their faces with every kind of sweet imaginable. One of Zac's gifts from Granny was a Stenchfinder. It was a huge fake nose made from rubber that was supposed to be able to sniff out lost objects. The others collapsed laughing when he put it on, but he made them all find a hiding place, eager to see if he could smell them out. It worked brilliantly. An hour later, after they'd all had a turn, they laughed and joked under the twinkling tree before passing out, exhausted.

Christmas Day passed in a blur, as is always the way when people are having such fun. With the exception of Mrs. Huggins, everyone was there: Tinn, Cornelius, Julius . . . even Rigby Sundown and his wolf, Maggie, had been invited. There were party games, and Christmas crackers that exploded like fireworks, and the feast was fantastic.

Zac piled his plate high with turkey and ham and little

sausages wrapped in smoked bacon. There was jelly and ice cream, and Christmas cake, and a flaming Christmas pudding that burned different colors. Tom gave Zac a bag of jelly snakes, and they wriggled all the way down to his belly.

After the meal, Mr. Huggins took Tom and Tilly to Sweet Dreams to visit their mother, who was awake and feeling much better. Everyone else decided that a nap was in order, and the room was soon full of snoring and belching.

Granny hadn't gone to sleep, though.

"Fancy a little walk?" she asked Zac.

"Why not?" he said.

"Where are we going?" he asked as Granny took him through the double doors to the abandoned corridor he knew so well.

"Just through here."

Granny opened the doors to the cavernous library and led him in. It was even larger than he remembered. There were books everywhere, reaching up into the darkness. The air was thick with dust.

"What's going on?" said Zac.

Granny smiled. "When I first became an apprentice," she said, "my father gave me a gift." She lifted the spare pair of spectacles from around her neck and unscrewed the magic arm. "These are what he gave me."

Zac stared at the glasses.

"I'd like to keep the tradition alive," she said. "So I have something for you."

She disappeared into the corridor and came back carrying a wooden box with small holes in the top. She set it gently on the floor.

"Go on, lad," she said. "Open it!"

Zac lifted the lid. Inside, curled up in some cozy bedding, was a tiny white wolf pup.

"Her name is Misty," said Granny. "Sundown suggested that a wolf might be the perfect gift. As a matter of fact, his Maggie is this little one's auntie. You must look after her. A wolf is the most loyal friend a person can ever have."

"Wow, thanks, Granny!" said Zac, and he scooped the pup up into his arms. She pawed at his face.

They stayed in the library for a while, playing with Misty. She skidded on the shiny floor, unable to grip with her tiny claws. Finally, Zac turned to Granny.

"We have to go back home soon, don't we?"

"Yes, lad," said Granny. "Tinn has set me a task, and it means we'll have to return to the Waking World."

"What sort of task?"

"That doesn't matter for now. Don't look so sad! You'll still be my apprentice. You'll still learn about magic and dreams and all the rest. And I'm sure you'll be seeing lots of your friends soon enough."

"But what about Nocturne?" Zac said. "Shouldn't we stay and help? I haven't seen a single Dream Stealer in my dreams for days. No Dream Stealers means no danger for the Waking World, and that's brilliant, but they're still out there. They'll be back, won't they?"

"I fear they will," said Granny. "They won't give up so easily. But for now, things are under control. There are more Knights than there have been in years. Tom and Tilly are ready to become more involved. Julius has been promoted from apprentice to full Knight. Tinn himself is training Noelle — he's certain he's discovered a real talent there. He's even hired Rigby Sundown to keep an eye on the Dream Plains. They'll all track down and turn in as many Dream Stealers as they can, you mark my words."

Zac was silent for a moment. "Granny," he began slowly, "what Mr. Tinn said . . . about the Trinity. What if it is *me* who's meant to stop the Dream Stealers —"

"Then all the more reason for keeping you safe in the Waking World," said Granny. "You need to learn more about your dream talent, to control it. And I've told you, I don't want to speak about that business. Not now. The Dream Stealers still believe I'm the danger, and I intend to keep it that way."

"But I'm scared that means they'll come for you," said Zac, staring at the floor.

Granny put her arm around him. "If they do, lad, I'll have them running straight back to the shadows they crawled out from! In any case, the most important thing here isn't *me* — it's stopping *them* from driving the Waking World mad with terrible dreams. That's something you *should* be afraid of."

"Maybe we already have stopped them," said Zac.

Granny smiled sadly. "You shouldn't be worrying about that today. It's Christmas! Come on, we should get back to the others. They'll be wondering where we've got to."

She stood up and walked back out into the empty corridor. Zac gazed around the library. Two weeks ago he hadn't known anything about this wondrous place.

Two weeks. It seemed like a lifetime.

The things he'd seen since then! And the enemies he'd battled! He'd fought a werewolf, and clashed with goblins and vampires and Dream Stealers. He'd soared through the clouds in an old camper van, and he'd escaped the clutches of evil skywaymen. He'd even found out that he had a special dream talent, and Granny was going to teach him all about magic.

Most important of all, for the first time in his life, he'd made friends. Real friends. The future was uncertain, but he knew they would face it together — he and Granny, Tom and Tilly, Rumpous Tinn and the Knights of Nod. They'd fight until the end, because they had something to fight for.

The sound of a booming guffaw drifted along the corridor. Zac smiled. Cornelius. Hugging Misty, he walked back toward the laughter of his friends.

And all around the Waking World, sleeping spirits passed through the mist, into the world of dreams.

Acknowledgments

Huge thanks to Barry, Imogen, Christine, Rachel, and everyone else at the fantastic Chicken House. By taking a chance on a little book about dreams, you have helped me achieve my own. I will never forget it.

Thanks to Janet, for falling in love with Zac from the very beginning. This will always be our story.

Thanks to my real-life heroes, Kenny and Lorna, who can always make me laugh.

And most important of all . . . thanks to Aileen, my beautiful, wonderful wife. If I had a magic compass, it would have led me to you.